WHEN the WAR CAME HOME

WHEN the WAR CAME HOME

LESLEY PARR

BLOOMSBURY
CHILDREN'S BOOKS
LONDON OXFORD NEW YORK NEW DELHI SYDNEY

BLOOMSBURY CHILDREN'S BOOKS
Bloomsbury Publishing Plc
50 Bedford Square, London WC1B 3DP, UK
29 Earlsfort Terrace, Dublin 2, Ireland

BLOOMSBURY, BLOOMSBURY CHILDREN'S BOOKS and the Diana logo
are trademarks of Bloomsbury Publishing Plc

First published in Great Britain in 2022 by Bloomsbury Publishing Plc

A catalogue record for this book is available from the British Library

ISBN: PB: 978-1-5266-2100-9; eBook: 978-1-5266-2099-6

2 4 6 8 10 9 7 5 3 1

Typeset by RefineCatch Limited, Bungay, Suffolk

Printed and bound in Great Britain by CPI Group (UK) Ltd, Croydon CR0 4YY

MIX
Paper from
responsible sources
FSC® C171272
www.fsc.org

To find out more about our authors and books visit www.bloomsbury.com
and sign up for our newsletters

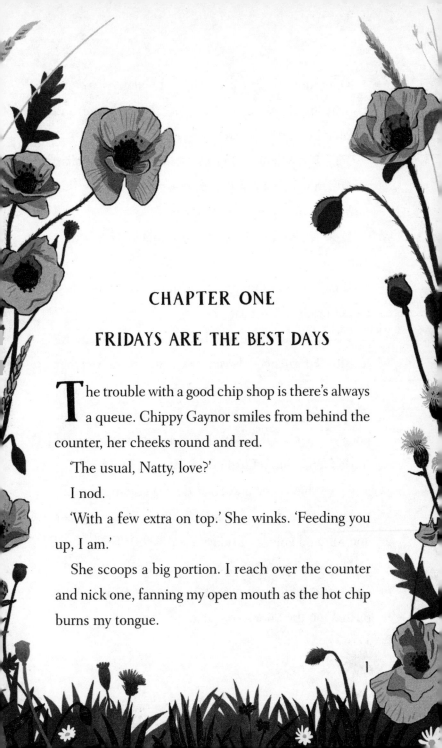

CHAPTER ONE

FRIDAYS ARE THE BEST DAYS

The trouble with a good chip shop is there's always a queue. Chippy Gaynor smiles from behind the counter, her cheeks round and red.

'The usual, Natty, love?'

I nod.

'With a few extra on top.' She winks. 'Feeding you up, I am.'

She scoops a big portion. I reach over the counter and nick one, fanning my open mouth as the hot chip burns my tongue.

1

'Duw, now there's a swish coat. New, is it?' she says, using tongs to pick up the cod in batter and plonk it on top of the steaming chips.

'Yes,' I say, smoothing my hand over the collar, careful not to touch it with the greasy fingers that picked up the chip. 'For my birthday.'

'Well you're a lucky dab.' She smiles. 'How's your mam?'

'Busy,' I say, thinking of all the extra hours she's worked to buy this coat.

'I know that feeling!' She grins, nodding at the queue. 'Fourpence please, love.' She holds out her plump hand. Chippy Gaynor's whole family is plump; you never go hungry if you have a chip shop. 'Your poor mam though. Gets his money's worth out of those factory girls, Litton does. Slave driver, he is.'

I pay, thank her and rush home, holding the fat, hot packet under my nose, breathing in newspaper and salt and vinegar. Fridays are the best days.

They don't have time to get cold – two doors down, above the ironmonger's and up some narrow stairs, I push open the door to our flat.

2

Mam's laying the table. There's three plates, one with bread and margarine on, and two glasses. Dandelion and burdock for me, stout for her. Friday night is for treats. No matter how bad things get, it's a tradition in our family. There are flowers in the bud vase in the middle of the table; they're only dog daisies picked from the lane, but they're pretty. Mam says Dad used to do it for her, but I was too small when he died to remember things like that. So now she does it for me and she always makes it nice.

'Chippy Gaynor gave us extra,' I say, kissing Mam's cheek and taking off my coat.

'Lovely.'

'I got the best bit of cod too.'

'Good girl.'

She's not looking at me, but I can see her eyes are red. She sighs as she shares out the chips. She must be tired. Like Gaynor said, Litton is a slave driver. I cut the fish not quite in half and give her the biggest end. She swaps it for the one on my plate as soon as I sit down.

'You're a growing girl. Now, tell me … how was school?'

'Good,' I say. 'We had boiled ham with potatoes and peas.'

She smiles. 'Funny how lessons are never the first thing you tell me about.'

I shrug. 'I'm a growing girl! Arithmetic was hard, singing was easy. We had jam roly-poly for pudding. I had seconds.'

Mam laughs but it looks a bit forced. She folds a piece of bread round some chips and licks the dripping margarine off her hand. 'Natty?' I look up. 'You know how, on Monday, Lorraine Marshall had to go to the doctor?'

I nod.

'Well, as if that didn't cost her enough, Litton docked her wages for the half-hour she was gone. Half an hour! Even after I made up her quota in my dinner break.'

'You never told me that.'

She takes a big bite of her butty so she doesn't have to answer.

'Why are you telling me this now?' I ask. 'You haven't done something, have you?'

4

'Why do you think I did something?'

'Because you always do, Mam.' She'll have stuck her nose in, gone on about workers' rights and fairness and, if she can manage to fit it in, votes for women too. Champion of the underdog, that's my mother.

'Well, Natty, people need to see a doctor if they're ill without the fear of losing money.' She looks at her plate. 'So I called a meeting today, to see what can be done about Litton … and … he sacked me.'

'He *what*?'

She puts down her knife and fork, and rubs her forehead. 'It's just not right how he treats people. He needs to understand how it is for us. For the workers.'

'But you always say he's never had to struggle for anything in his life! He inherited that factory, so why would he listen now? It's pointless.'

'Standing up for what you believe in is never pointless. Especially now. The war is over. It's the twenties, things are changing.'

'But the only thing that changed was you getting the sack.'

5

'Eat your tea before it gets cold.'

I slowly peel the batter off my fish, not looking at her.

'There's something else,' Mam says. 'But it's going to be all right because I have a plan.' She takes a big breath. 'If we can't find the rent this week, Mr Tipton will throw us out ... I ... I got a bit behind, see.'

Oh no, not again. I don't want to move *again*.

'How? How can you get behind? You always say a roof over our heads is more important than anything!' I point to the fish and chips. 'Why would you give me money for this if we didn't have the rent?'

Mam's quiet. She's looking at her and Dad's wedding photograph on the cabinet. Friday night supper was something else Dad used to do. That's why. But things have been tight before – why is it so bad this time? Her eyes move to my coat hanging on the hook by the door.

And suddenly I'm furious. But not with her, with myself. If I hadn't stopped outside Nicholls every time we passed, looking up at that coat in the window, if I hadn't grown so fast and always had extra helpings

6

of school dinners, I'd still be in my old coat. It would have patched. We could have let the seams out again.

'We can take it back,' I whisper, the words scratching over the lump in my throat. 'My coat, we can take it back.'

'It won't be enough, sweetheart.'

'So you picked a fight with Litton, when it wasn't even your fight to have, when you knew we were behind on the rent?'

'Lorraine Marshall's got her girl home with the babies, her being a war widow. But, Natty –' she leans across the table – 'Like I said, I have a plan. We won't be out on the street. I wrote to your Aunty Mary and Uncle Dewi last week.'

'Why?'

'When your dad died, they were good to us. They've always said if we need anything, I only have to ask.'

'Ask for what? Not money! Mam, that's shaming!'

'No, no. Not money. Just a place to stay until I can find a new job—'

'*But don't they live in Ynysfach?*' I drop my fork and it clatters on the plate. Mam winces.

'Yes, love, that's where we're going. I got a letter back this morning.'

I frown. 'And you wrote to them *last week*? But you lost your job today?'

Mam shuffles in her seat. 'I knew it was coming. Litton was just looking for a way to get rid of me.'

'And you gave him one. You knew we were behind on the rent and you still had to make trouble!'

Mam looks at her plate for a few seconds, then pushes her chair back. 'I'm going for a walk.'

'But your food!'

'I'll have it after.'

'Cold?' I say. 'Because there's not enough coal to heat the oven. Lorraine Marshall can look after herself, Mam. What about us?'

She doesn't look at me, just leaves me at the table.

'What about *us*?' I shout after her, but she's gone.

So much for Fridays being the best days.

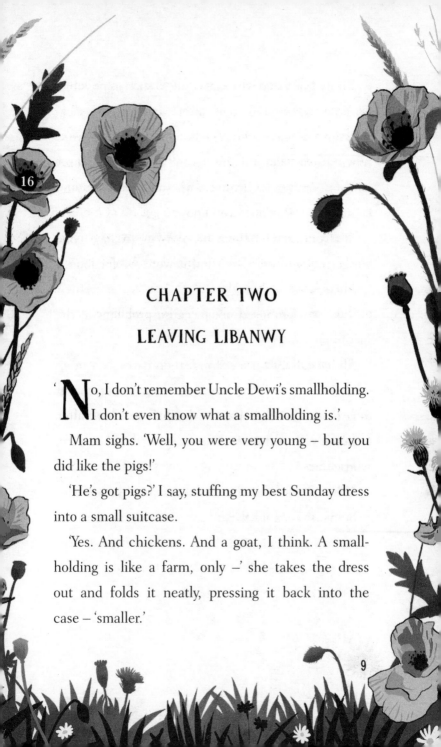

CHAPTER TWO

LEAVING LIBANWY

'No, I don't remember Uncle Dewi's smallholding. I don't even know what a smallholding is.'

Mam sighs. 'Well, you were very young – but you did like the pigs!'

'He's got pigs?' I say, stuffing my best Sunday dress into a small suitcase.

'Yes. And chickens. And a goat, I think. A small-holding is like a farm, only –' she takes the dress out and folds it neatly, pressing it back into the case – 'smaller.'

Aunty Mary said we must come as soon as possible. So here we are, four days after Mam got the sack, packing up our things. Again. But this time we're moving away from Libanwy – and my school and my friends – and going to live with smelly animals and some relatives I don't even know.

'It's very kind of them to allow us to stay while we get back on our feet, and it won't be for long. I promise.'

'Like you promised not to cause problems at the factory?'

She goes stiff for a second, then carries on in an even jollier voice. 'You won't get to see your cousin Sara though, she's a maid in Cardiff now, but Huw's at home still, and Nerys is your age – that'll be nice, won't it?'

Why do grown-ups always think you'll get on with people just because they're the same age as you?

Mam sighs again and closes the lid of the case. 'Sit on this, will you? It'll never close otherwise.'

I thud down on it, extra hard.

*

I wish we didn't have to walk past the factory to get to the bus stop. And that the bus wasn't going at the end of the factory dinner break, because there are all Mam's old workmates, standing on the steps waiting to go back in.

We try to hurry past but it's no use. A woman in a blue headscarf steps out of the little crowd, pointing at our suitcases. It's Lorraine Marshall.

'Ffion, is this because of me?' she asks.

Mam slows but keeps walking.

'No, Lorraine. It was a long time coming.'

The factory doors open and there's Dennis Litton, looking like a smug cockerel. He scans the crowd until his eyes rest on Mam. 'You no longer work here, Mrs Lydiate. You need to remove yourself from my premises.'

'I'm not on your premises,' Mam says, stepping forward so her toe is right on the edge of where the steps start.

Oh Mam, what are you doing?

'If *this lot* want to put up with your tyranny –' she nods towards the factory girls but keeps her eyes on him – 'more fool them. Me? I'm glad to see the back of you.'

The bus is pulling up, so I run and get the driver to wait. Mam strolls across the road, her head held high.

'She won't be a minute now,' I say.

The driver turns around in his seat. 'What's going on there then?'

'Nothing.'

I climb the steps, annoyed with myself for feeling a little bit proud of her when I'm supposed to be cross.

I stare out of the window as we bounce along the long road to Ynysfach. The tree-covered drop into the valley is so deep I can't see the river at the bottom. And then we're climbing even higher, the driver forcing his bus up and up over the mountain. Up and down, up and down, all the way to Uncle Dewi's.

Mam offers me a crumpled paper bag. 'Mint humbug?'

I take one. 'Thanks.'

'Oh, you're speaking to me then?'

I look away and roll my eyes. She keeps on. 'It's a nice afternoon for a bus ride.'

She's trying to make the best of it, but I'm not going to join in and treat this like some sort of jaunt. We've just left the nicest flat we've ever lived in and the only village I know. And it's all her fault.

'I remember Nerys now,' I say, glancing at her. Before she can answer I add, 'She was annoying.'

I pop the humbug in my mouth, fold my arms and look out of the window again.

Two more humbugs later, the bus pulls up opposite some bushes and flowerbeds set behind railings. There's a sign saying *Ynysfach Park*.

'Must be our stop,' Mam says. We shuffle along the aisle with our cases and step down on to the pavement, just as a nurse and two soldiers in Hospital Blues and khaki caps come towards us. The nurse is pushing one in a wheelchair; the other is really young, not much older than me. Almost too young to have fought in the war. And too young to look so sad. He's very fair, in a gingery-blond sort of way, even his eyelashes are pale. I realise my suitcase is in the way of the wheelchair so I go to move it just as the younger soldier reaches out as if to help. But his hand shakes and shakes, so he pulls it back. We lock eyes for a second that feels like forever; like we're both unsure what to do next. There's something about the way he is. It's like how I feel.

Lost.

'It's all right, I've got it,' I say as the others and Mam say hello, then the soldiers and nurse cross the road over to the park.

A passenger calls out for the bus to get a move on, and the driver leans out of his seat and glowers up the aisle. 'Have some respect, mun!' Then he faces the road again and makes a salute before pulling off.

Mam looks around. 'I don't think this is right, there are meant to be shops. We must have got off too early.'

I huff, but say nothing, just pick up my suitcase and trudge down the hill.

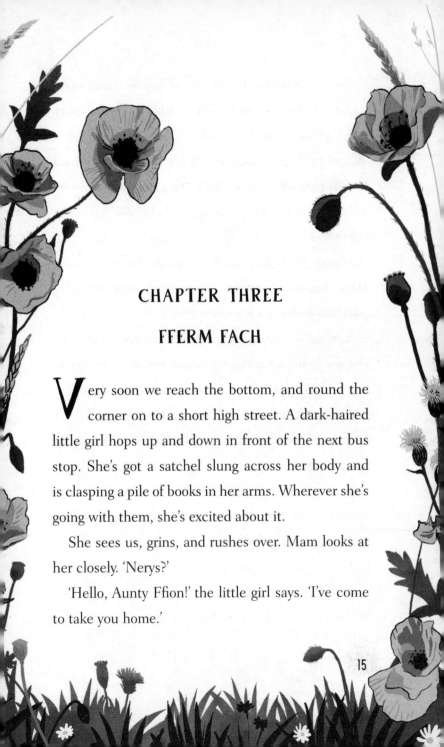

CHAPTER THREE

FFERM FACH

Very soon we reach the bottom, and round the corner on to a short high street. A dark-haired little girl hops up and down in front of the next bus stop. She's got a satchel slung across her body and is clasping a pile of books in her arms. Wherever she's going with them, she's excited about it.

She sees us, grins, and rushes over. Mam looks at her closely. 'Nerys?'

'Hello, Aunty Ffion!' the little girl says. 'I've come to take you home.'

15

Come to take us home? She makes us sound like a couple of strays. Which is a bit too close to the truth.

Nerys smiles at me. Now I look at her properly, she's older than I first thought. But she's so small it's hard to tell. Her hair is cut into a short bob and her eyes are really dark and really intense. 'Did you get off at the wrong stop? Loads of people do that! Did you know it was me?' Before I can answer, she goes on. 'You didn't, did you? I can tell from your faces. I imagine you thought I was a younger girl, ten maybe, or perhaps even eight – some people think I'm only eight.' She lifts the hem of her dress to show grey woollen stockings and heavy black boots. 'Short legs, see.'

Mam's trying not to smile. I'm just hoping I don't have to share a bedroom with this cousin. I'll never get any peace.

'Sorry I can't help with the cases. I have all these books to carry because I'm getting a scholarship to the Brecon County School. And don't worry, I know it looks like we're going up the Gweld but we're not really.'

'What's the Gweld?' I ask.

'That.' Nerys shifts the books in her arms and uses

her elbow to point at the biggest mountain. 'It's not its proper name but it's what everyone round here calls it.' She stomps off like a miniature carthorse. 'Follow me!'

So we follow. On the other side of the road is a school, smaller than mine, one storey with railings all around the yard. YSGOL YNYSFACH 1894 is carved into the stone above the door. On our side there's a corner shop, a bakery, a newsagent, a butcher and the Post Office at the end.

Along the high street we go, then up a sloping road, past terraced houses that look just like the ones in Libanwy. Me and Mam trail behind, listening to Nerys pointing out everything along the way, from their chapel to where her teacher lives.

'Behind those streets down there is Talbot House. Before the war, it was a big, posh house but they needed an auxiliary hospital so now it's that. If you see soldiers around the village, that's where they'll be from.' She nods to a big open space on the Gweld. 'And sometimes we go up there for picnics. It's a bit slopey but that just makes it especially good for rolling down.' She glances back at me. 'I mostly go with Owen. He's my friend. You'll like him, Natty, he's funny and kind and really good at rugby.'

She turns away again and I go to pull a face at Mam, but she's watching Nerys and smiling. 'Isn't she a delight?'

Delight? My dim memory of an annoying cousin is proving to be true.

A few people pass us and some say hello; one woman even stops to chat. 'You must be Mary and Dewi's family from Libanwy. I'm Hannah.'

'Did you see the bakery down the bottom, opposite the school?' Nerys says to me and Mam, bouncing on her tiptoes. 'That's Hannah's shop, that is.' She beams up at Hannah. 'This is my cousin Natty and my Aunty Ffion. I'm calling her aunty, but really she's my father's cousin so that makes her my first cousin, once removed, and Natty is my second cousin but I'll just say she's my cousin. To make it simple.'

That was *simple*? I put down my suitcase and rub my aching arm.

Hannah laughs. 'Well, whatever you are, any

18

relation of the Williamses is a friend to me. You get Mary to bring you down for a cuppa one day.'

Mam looks really pleased. 'That would be lovely, thank you.'

'We'd better go,' Nerys says. 'Pigs won't feed themselves – Huw'll go mad if he has to do it again.'

'Nice to meet you both,' Hannah says. 'You'll soon settle in. Friendly place, this is.' And off she goes down the hill.

On the corner of one street is a chip shop, windows open, the smell of hot oil drifting towards us. I used to love that smell, but now it's only a reminder of how Fridays are going to be very different. We keep walking until there aren't as many houses and it feels a bit more like the countryside. From this point on the hill, to our right down below, is a big flat space – a playing field, yellow flowers near a bowling green, and a playground with swings and a slide. And I can see the nurse and the soldiers, their Hospital Blues standing out against all the green.

After about fifteen minutes, Nerys nattering all the way, we reach a little track. At the end of it, over some trees, is a roof and a smoking chimney. Nerys announces that's their house. Up we go and, when we get to the top, I see it's old, and has a sort of tired-but-loved look about it. There's a yard with wooden pens, a small barn and other outbuildings. I can hear the goat bleating.

I try to remember being here before, but I can't.

'That's our orchard,' Nerys says, pointing right across the yard to a small gate set in a tall hedge.

'Oh, the orchard,' Mam says, all wide-eyed like she's never seen an apple before. 'I'd forgotten about that.'

A sign on the gate says *Fferm Fach*. 'Little Farm'. Nerys opens it and waves me through. 'Got to close it properly, see. Best if I do it.'

I don't know why she's making out it's something special, it's just an ordinary gate latch, not tricky at all. I go to say so, but Mam must guess because she whispers, '*No*, Natty.'

So this is it then. Another makeshift life. One where I can't open my mouth and Nerys never shuts hers.

CHAPTER FOUR

HUW

'Maaaaaaam!' Nerys shouts across the yard. 'I've got them! The bus was on time for a change.'

A woman comes out of a door on the side of the house. She looks like Nerys, with her round face and dark hair.

'Hello, hello!' she calls, wiping floury hands on her pinny. 'Ffion! Natty! It's lovely to see you – it's been so long!' She takes Mam's hand in both of hers and squeezes. 'Oops, excuse the flour. I'm baking.'

'Not on our account, I hope?' Mam says.

21

'It's fine.' Aunty Mary smiles. 'If we can't make something nice to welcome you into our home, then what's the world coming to?'

Mam looks happy, but I feel even more like a charity case. Aunty Mary turns to me. 'And this must be our Natty! Well, aren't you a picture? Come in, come in, let's get you both settled, then we can have a cuppa.'

The kitchen is really big, warm and welcoming. It's got a huge wooden table in the middle, and the floor is made of red and black tiles. There's a Welsh dresser, its shelves full of plates and cups. I can tell Mam's admiring it. She's always wanted one. On the hob, there's a bakestone and, on the worktop next to it, piles of speckled discs.

Welsh cakes.

'I'll just put these books in our bedroom out of the way,' Nerys says. 'I'll be back now in a minute.'

Our bedroom. We're sharing then. Marvellous!

Mam and Aunty Mary chat like old friends. I feel silly standing here, so slip back out to the yard. I go over to the pigsty, and straight away two of them come up to the fence. There's a gate the other side of it that leads on to a paddock where I suppose they can run around. If pigs *can* run. I've never thought about it before. These two are big, with dirty, wet snouts and ears that flop over their eyes. They're sweeter than I thought they'd be. I lean over to pat one of them.

'*Don't!*'

I spin around and slip, landing on the dusty ground. I look up to see an older boy frowning down at me and holding out a hand. I take it and let go as soon as I'm up. My hands and coat are filthy.

'You can't go sticking your hand in with the pigs, mun!' he says, obviously trying not to laugh. 'They'll have your fingers off, they will.'

My cheeks burn hot. 'I was only going to stroke them.'

'Why? They're not dogs.'

'Huw!' Nerys flies across the yard and into the boy's arms. He swings her around.

'Well?' he says, setting her down again. 'What did you get?'

'A hundred out of a hundred in spellings and one

23

wrong in times tables,' she says. 'I was cross about that, but Ivy Beynon got her sevens all muddled up so that made me feel better.'

'Nerys!' He seems like he wants to tell her off but he's laughing. 'It wasn't eight times seven again, was it?'

'Yes,' she huffs. 'It won't stick in my brain. Oh, Natty – what happened to you?'

'Tried to feed herself to the pigs,' the boy says. I could kick him, but I might fall over again.

He's tall and thin, nothing like Nerys's shape at all, but they have the same intense, dark eyes.

'He's older than me,' she says, as if I can't see this for myself. 'My sister is too. Sara. She's sixteen and he's seventeen. Mam and Dad thought they'd finished with babies but then I came along.' She spins around with her arms out. 'Dad says I was a *lovely surprise*.'

Huw laughs again. 'You could say that.'

'You finished for the day?' she asks him.

He glances at a wooden outbuilding that sits between the barn and the tall orchard hedge. 'For now, yeah.'

Nerys pulls two sugary Welsh cakes out of her smock pocket and offers one to me. 'They're still warm. Mam doesn't know I took them.' She grins. 'Don't tell or she'll have my guts for garters.'

I hold up my hands, showing all the dirt.

'Oh,' Nerys says. 'You need a wash.'

'Where's mine then?' Huw asks.

Nerys looks uncertain, but offers her Welsh cake to him anyway.

'Nah, don't be daft. I'll pinch my own.'

Huw's teasing her just like he teased me. This might be his peculiar way of welcoming me to the family.

We walk back inside together. He goes straight to the big table and puts jam on a Welsh cake. I can hear Mam and Aunty Mary moving about upstairs.

'Here, Natty,' Nerys says, opening a door into a small room. 'You can wash in the scullery.'

'Yeah, before you develop swine fever,' Huw says.

Nerys must see the alarmed look on my face because she says, 'Take no notice, he's only pulling your leg. Rotten thing.' She clips him round the head and they both grin.

The scullery smells of soap and, as I wash my hands and wipe down my coat, I look around at the boxes, basins and jugs on the shelves. They have a lot more things than me and Mam do.

Loud noises come from the kitchen, rattling and slamming. Huw says, *'Damn it,'* and Nerys speaks in almost-whispers. I peep from the doorway.

'Just leave me alone, will you?' Huw shouts. 'I can shut a flaming drawer by myself!'

He's pushing and shoving at a dresser drawer; it's at an angle, and he's going to break it if he keeps on. Nerys's hands are twitching, like she's desperate to help but knows she'll only make things worse.

'It's jammed now,' Huw mutters. 'Stupid thing!'

He pulls it with such force that it flies out of his hands and hits the floor tiles with a smashing, clattering sound. He turns to Nerys and she flinches. It's horrible to see.

'There,' he says, breathing hard, his voice low. 'See how useless I am?'

He goes through to the living room, slamming the door behind him. Heavy footsteps thud on the stairs above my head. What the heck just happened? They were the best of friends just now, joking about pigs.

I dry my hands and go into the kitchen. Nerys is on the floor with her back to me. The drawer's next to her, and she's putting back the things which must have fallen out of it. Then she stands, slides it smoothly and easily into the dresser and, for a few seconds, the only thing that moves is her shoulders as she takes deep breaths.

'Are you all right?' I ask.

She jumps, and wipes her face before she turns around. 'He doesn't mean it. He's not the same since he came back.'

'Back from where?'

Nerys looks at me like I'm stupid. 'The war,' she says. 'It's not his fault.'

'I thought he was seventeen?'

'He is.' She frowns. 'He lied about his age. Disappeared and sent us a letter from Chelsea Barracks. Mam cried for weeks. Dad tried to get him

27

back – took his birth certificate to the recruiting office and everything – but he was already on his way to Belgium by then.' She sighs. 'He was fourteen at Passchendaele.'

Passchendaele. My cousin was in one of the biggest battles of the war and I didn't know.

Nerys pulls out a chair and waves for me to sit, then takes the one next to me. She pushes the jam pot across the table. 'It's nice,' she says. 'Sara makes it out of wimberries from up the Gweld.'

I think that means she doesn't want to talk about Huw any more, which is fine with me. I take a Welsh cake but shake my head at the jam. 'I like mine plain, but thanks.'

'*Nerys! Pigs!*' Huw's voice carries from upstairs. He still sounds angry.

She stands quickly. 'I'd better get on with it. You can go up to our room if you like. It's at the top of the second staircase.'

I bite into my Welsh cake, I've never had one with such juicy currants.

CHAPTER FIVE

IT'S WAR, ISN'T IT?

Nerys's room – *our room*, she called it – is right up in the eaves of the attic, small but cosy. There's a metal-framed bed with a patchwork quilt, a chest of drawers, some shelves, and a little desk and chair squeezed under the sloping ceiling near the window. Nerys has a lot of books. They're piled everywhere. But still, there's space on one of the shelves; a folded sheet of paper stands on it, like a greetings card. I step closer to see lots of flowers scruffily drawn around the words:

Natty's shelf

I go over to the chest of drawers, and there's one open; inside is another flowery note:

Natty's drawer

I can't help but smile. But what I can't see is *Natty's bed*. And no room to fit one in either. Then I notice a lump at the bottom end of Nerys's. I lift the quilt. Another pillow. So we're topping and tailing then – oh, great! Her feet in my face all night.

I go over to the window. There she is, feeding the pigs, talking to them, looking sad. I suppose it's because of her brother. First the soldier at the bus stop and now Huw. The war ended ages ago, but it feels like it hasn't really gone away. We had three in Libanwy who didn't come home. There's a memorial in the chapel.

Nerys pats the pigs on their heads – just like Huw told me not to – and turns to the house. She sees me and waves, smiling again – happy to have me here. Willing to share what she's got. I feel a twinge of guilt.

I wave back and start to unpack my things. The door creaks and I turn to see Mam's head poking around the frame. 'What a lovely room!' She comes in. 'You've always wanted an attic bedroom, haven't you?'

'Of my own, yeah,' I mutter, shutting the drawer hard and straight away thinking of Huw again.

'Oh, and look at that!' She lifts the note off the shelf. 'How kind!'

Yes, Nerys *is* kind. She's welcomed us and made room for me. But that doesn't mean she's not annoying.

'Ffion?' Aunty Mary calls up the stairs. 'If that offer of helping with supper still stands, I could do with some carrots peeling.'

'You'd better go, Mam,' I say, putting my nightdress under my pillow.

She sighs, and kisses me on the forehead. 'We just have to make the best of it, love. It's not forever.'

I've just packed the last thing away when there's

the thump of running feet and Nerys bursts through the door.

'Do you like it? It's a nice bedroom, isn't it? Dad said I could have Sara's room now she's away but I said I prefer this one. Anyway, Aunty Ffion's got that now. Sara gets one weekend off a month, but if you're still here that won't matter, we can all fit in. Did you see your notes? I tried to draw flowers but I'm not very good at art – not like Huw. That's all right though as it's not on the entrance exam for the Brecon County School.' She throws herself on the bed and laughs breathlessly. 'I just ran all the way up.'

I have no idea what to say.

'I'm glad you're staying,' she goes on. 'I miss Sara. Which is strange, as whenever she *is* around we fight like ferrets in a sack. I suppose that's sisters for you though, isn't it?'

'I don't know,' I say. 'It's just me and Mam.'

'But I do have the best big brother there is,' she says, like it's an actual fact, which surprises me after the way he spoke to her.

'What happened to him?' I ask. 'In Passchendaele, I mean.'

Nerys kneels on the bed and, with her back to me, rearranges some books on the shelf. 'I don't know. It's war, isn't it?'

Even though he works in a factory, Uncle Dewi must spend a lot of time on the smallholding because he's got a look of someone who stays out in all weathers. He's nice, with a kind smile, but if I have to hear one more time how proud he is of his 'brave, outspoken cousin', I'll explode. He's the union rep at his factory and as keen on workers' rights as Mam. Which is the last thing we need. He'll only make her worse.

'You're a lucky girl, Natty,' Uncle Dewi says. 'Having a mother like Ffion.'

I stab a carrot before nodding and smiling like a simpleton. *Yeah, I felt really lucky when she got the sack and we lost our home.*

'Bit shy, is it?' he says, nodding towards me. 'She doesn't get that from you, Ffion.'

'She's not usually quiet,' Mam answers, frowning.

'Roasties are lovely and crispy, Mam,' Huw says, glancing at me. I think he's trying to change the subject and I feel a rush of gratitude towards him.

But Uncle Dewi keeps on. 'When we got your letter, we said straight away that you must come here until you're back on your feet, didn't we, Mary? Plenty of room here for a revolutionary!'

He laughs. So do Mam, Aunty Mary and Nerys. But not me and Huw.

'Tell us again what you said to your boss on the steps this morning, Aunty Ffion!' Nerys says, bouncing in her seat.

Huw doesn't join in with the 'We love Ffion' chatter. All through the meal he's been friendly enough. Not like he was with the pigs, all full of jokes, but not crashing around and cursing either. More like he's on the outside of everything.

'Well, that was lovely,' Uncle Dewi says, mopping gravy with a big culf of bread. 'I was famished.'

Nerys gasps. 'Dad! You can't say that! We don't know what it's like to be really hungry – that's right isn't it, Mam? Not like Owen.' She looks to me. 'His

34

family never really have enough to eat. They don't have much money, see.'

I glance at Mam. When I was eight, and she lost her job in the laundry, we didn't have money for coal for a whole week. Every meal was bread and margarine. Some nights, I don't think Mam had anything at all, even though she said she did.

Aunty Mary lets out a big sigh. 'We'd feed him here anytime – but he's too proud to come. I doubt he's ever had a meal like this.'

I think of that last jam roly-poly. 'Not ever? Not even for his school dinner?'

Nerys screws her face up. 'School dinner?'

I nod, reaching for my glass of milk. 'We have lovely stews and dumplings, and the puddings are—'

'*At school?*'

'Yes, that's what I said.' For someone who's meant to be clever, she's being quite twp.

'We don't. We come home. That's why it's hard for families like Owen's who already don't have enough to go round.' Nerys frowns, licking gravy off her knife. 'So who pays for these dinners at your school?'

'No one! They're free!'

'*Free?*' she says, sitting up straight, her dark eyes even more intense. 'Then where are *our* dinners?'

I shrug, and look at Mam.

'It's up to each individual council as to whether they provide them or not.'

'But that's not fair!' Nerys squeals.

She's right, it isn't fair, but sometimes that's just the way things are.

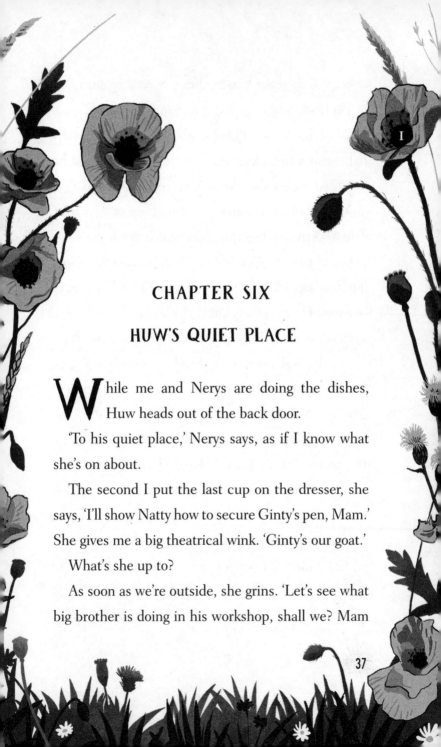

CHAPTER SIX

HUW'S QUIET PLACE

While me and Nerys are doing the dishes, Huw heads out of the back door.

'To his quiet place,' Nerys says, as if I know what she's on about.

The second I put the last cup on the dresser, she says, 'I'll show Natty how to secure Ginty's pen, Mam.' She gives me a big theatrical wink. 'Ginty's our goat.'

What's she up to?

As soon as we're outside, she grins. 'Let's see what big brother is doing in his workshop, shall we? Mam

37

says I should leave him be, but a peep can't hurt.'

Oh heck.

I look up at the biggest outbuilding, where yellow light shines through the open doors. I suppose if he *did* mind, he'd close them. And I am curious …

Me and Nerys watch from behind one of the doors. The workshop is big, but cluttered. Every surface has pots and jars and tins and crockery, some with closed lids, but lots with brushes and pencils sticking out of the top. There are rags and cloths, and a chair at a desk which is covered in sponges and more tin cans.

On the walls are tools, fixed into special places, like hammers and chisels in a shed … only they're different, smaller, and I have no idea what they're for. Stacked up on the floor, leaning against a wall, are flat rectangles covered in large cloths. And, in the middle of the workshop, an easel.

'Huw's a painter?' I whisper. I've never known anyone who actually paints before.

Nerys nods. 'Not just paint – he makes all sorts of pictures. He's brilliant at everything. I know I would say that because I'm his sister, but he is – honest!'

But Huw's not painting now. He's washing brushes at the sink in the corner.

She speaks even more quietly. 'And it helps him with all the horrible things he saw in the war. He says concentrating on the pictures is good because he doesn't think about anything else.'

This feels wrong. Snooping on him when he wanted to be on his own. Nerys said this was his quiet place. And if he was that angry over shutting a drawer, what's he going to be like if he catches us here?

'Let's go,' I say.

'In a minute.' Nerys shakes my hand off her shoulder and my knuckles scrape the door.

'Oww!'

Huw turns. We freeze. He laughs. 'You can come in, mun, you don't have to lurk like incompetent spies.'

Aunty Mary was wrong then. He doesn't mind at all.

We go inside.

It's woody and oily and dusty and warm; it's like the best shed smell mixed with paints. It's lovely.

There's an unfinished painting on the easel. Two pigs in their sty.

'Told you he was brilliant, didn't I?' Nerys beams.

'It's your welcoming committee,' he says to me, his dark eyes shining with mischief.

'Very funny,' I say.

'Can Natty see some of your other paintings?' Nerys asks, reaching to pull a cloth off the nearest rectangle. 'Is this the one of the Gweld?'

'Don't,' Huw says. 'It's not right yet.'

Nerys shakes her head. 'He's a true artist,' she says. 'Won't let us look at anything until it's perfect.'

'Look, it's too dark to see properly now anyway. Come another day, eh?' He pushes her gently out of the door. 'These things are best in the daylight, get the full effect.'

'Oh, all right,' she says grumpily. 'Nos da then.' She offers him her cheek, which he kisses, and heads back to the house.

I follow, but before I go into the kitchen, I glance back at Huw standing in front of the easel. He's a hard one to work out, but I think I like him. He's quite funny when he's not cross. A few days here might not be so bad after all.

40

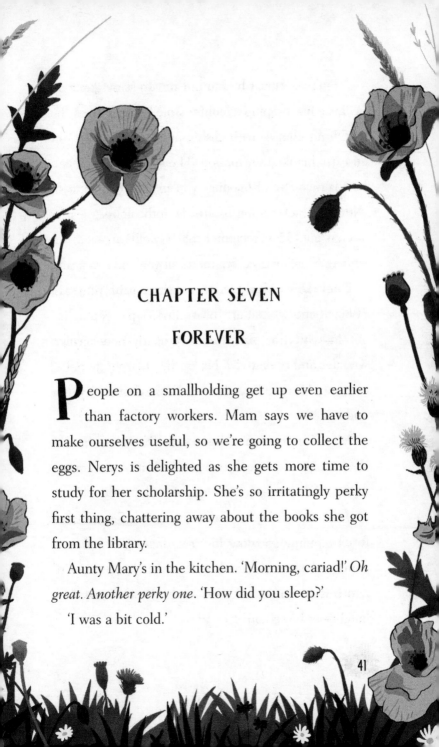

CHAPTER SEVEN

FOREVER

People on a smallholding get up even earlier than factory workers. Mam says we have to make ourselves useful, so we're going to collect the eggs. Nerys is delighted as she gets more time to study for her scholarship. She's so irritatingly perky first thing, chattering away about the books she got from the library.

Aunty Mary's in the kitchen. 'Morning, cariad!' *Oh great. Another perky one.* 'How did you sleep?'

'I was a bit cold.'

I don't say that I had to put my dressing gown on because her flipping daughter stole all the covers.

'Oh no, that won't do,' she says, frowning. 'I'll put an extra blanket out for you. The kettle's on. You can have a nice cup of tea once you've helped your mam with the chickens. She's already in the coop.'

I go out. Mam's behind the barn, I can hear her singing. Singing! Like the world's all jolly and rosy again.

Uncle Dewi's in the pigsty holding a squirming ball of black-and-white fluff. 'Mary, look! Davey's pup has got in with the pigs again.' A little Border collie wriggles and tries to lick his face.

Aunty Mary follows me out. We look at each other and laugh.

'It's not funny,' Uncle Dewi says. 'It's had its face in the trough – look at the state of it! Un-flaming-believable! Good job the pigs are in the paddock!'

'Then there's no harm done, is there?' She reaches for the puppy and looks into its face. 'Sid Davey is going to have a very hard time training you if you're this mischievous, isn't he? Yes he is. Ooh, who's a handsome boy then?'

'Don't talk to it like it's a baby, mun,' Uncle Dewi says. 'You'll only encourage it.' He sighs. 'The gate was open again.'

Aunty Mary buries her face in the dog's fur. I go up to them and stroke its head.

'We can't keep ignoring this,' Uncle Dewi says, glancing at me like he's uneasy. 'One day the pigs will get out and run amok! What if they got into the house?'

'He doesn't mean to, he just gets distracted more easily these days.'

'Then he needs help.'

'He's had help – doctors and tests and questions. He's got us and he's got time. That's enough.'

They're talking about Huw. They must be.

Aunty Mary takes the pup and walks towards the house. 'Don't listen to grumpy old Dewi. Let's see what we've got in the cupboard for you, eh?'

'Don't feed it, Mary!' he calls, shaking his head. 'Duw yn ol, we'll never get rid of it!'

I rummage around inside the chicken coop, collecting eggs, while Mam scatters grain in their little yard.

The hens cluck and peck and strut. I put an egg in the basket at my feet.

'Throw it over there, Mam,' I say. I don't like their beady eyes or sharp beaks.

'All right, love, but you're going to have to get used to them.'

'Not really,' I say. 'We'll be back in Libanwy soon, won't we?' I feel around in the straw and find another egg. 'When you get a new job.'

She does a surprised laugh. 'Natty, what on earth makes you think we can go back there?'

'Because it's our home. And you said this wouldn't be forever.'

'I meant we won't be living *here*, in this house, forever.' Mam stops throwing the grain. 'I thought you'd realise. Uncle Dewi's trying to get me a job in his factory. He's a supervisor now. Mary's taking Nerys to school today to ask the headmaster if you can have a place there.'

'What?' I stand and stare at her, the egg still warm in my hand.

'Well, you can't stay here all day every day – education

44

is important. And Nerys can introduce you to everyone. A girl like her must have lots of friends.'

'I wouldn't bet on it,' I mutter. Then, louder, 'But Mam, I've *got* friends. *In Libanwy.*'

She doesn't look at me, just keeps throwing grain. 'We're not going back.'

My fingers press around the egg.

'Look, love,' she says, in that voice she always uses to try to convince me she's right. 'Your aunty and uncle have said we can stay as long as we need to. Once I've saved up, we can find a nice flat, maybe even a house this time—'

'*In Ynysfach?*' My voice comes out high.

'Yes ... in Ynysfach. No – wait – hear me out. It'll be good for us to have family around.' She sighs. 'I'm sorry, but this is the way it has to be.'

'Because of *you*!' I'm tamping now, not caring what I say. 'Like the time you argued with Mrs Wallis because she didn't want to be a suffragette!'

'Stupid woman didn't even *want* to vote.'

'She still can't vote, Mam! She's too poor – and neither can you! Don't you understand? You keep saying

45

things are changing for the better, but not for us!'

'Love, please …' She rests a hand on my arm. I shake it off.

'Because we had to leave Mrs Wallis's and live over a stinking fishmonger, no one would sit next to me at school. They said I smelt fishy.'

You did not smell fishy! I keep you clean and tidy, no matter what.'

'No matter what,' I say quietly. There's a cracking, crunching sound as the egg breaks. Horrible stickiness drips between my fingers. I wipe it on my apron.

'But, Natty, I never knew. You never said.'

'No, because you're always too busy with your next fight to worry about me. Always a sad case to find justice for. Well, guess who the sad cases really are, Mam?'

I turn and run. She calls after me but I don't look back. I undo the straps of my apron with struggling fingers, pull it off and fling it to the ground.

And I keep running. Away from the hens, through the yard, out of the gate and down the track. She doesn't follow me. I don't know if that makes me feel better or worse.

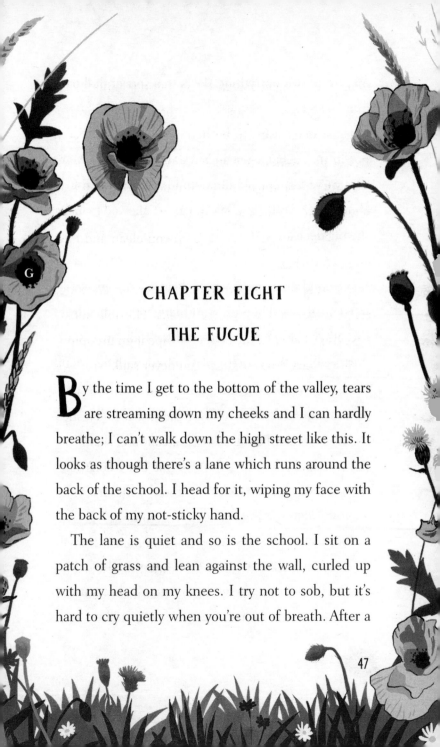

CHAPTER EIGHT

THE FUGUE

B y the time I get to the bottom of the valley, tears are streaming down my cheeks and I can hardly breathe; I can't walk down the high street like this. It looks as though there's a lane which runs around the back of the school. I head for it, wiping my face with the back of my not-sticky hand.

The lane is quiet and so is the school. I sit on a patch of grass and lean against the wall, curled up with my head on my knees. I try not to sob, but it's hard to cry quietly when you're out of breath. After a

47

minute or two everything slows to a sort of dull pain in my chest.

I just don't want to be here. Not in Fferm Fach, not in that school, not in Ynysfach at all. But Mam says we've left our old life behind and what can I do about that? Nothing. Children aren't allowed to make the big decisions.

Some children come down the lane, eyeing me warily, but I turn away. Shouting and laughter comes from the other side of the wall – school's about to start. Nerys will be there, in the playground, with her friend Owen. I must have sat here for ages. The bell goes. Then it's quiet. I get up and walk, following the curve of the lane. I wander around, turn back down the high street, look in the shop windows and try to find things to like in Ynysfach.

And it's quite nice; it really is.

But it's not home.

I stop to look at the bread and cakes in the bakery window. Someone waves from behind the counter. It's Hannah, the woman we met on the hill. I forgot that Nerys said this is her shop. I wave back and carry on, not knowing where I'm wandering. I keep going. On my left, behind railings, are lots of bushes and flowers. The park. A bit further along, the gates are open. At the top of the sloping path I hear voices and clapping and make out flashes of white; there must be a bowls match on. I'll watch that for a while.

The bowling pavilion is pretty, like a little railway station, all painted wood, and bright and fresh against the yellow of the daffodils. One person watches from a bench at the far side of the green: a fair-haired lad in Hospital Blues. The young soldier from yesterday. The nurse and the man in the wheelchair are on the pavilion patio.

The man grins and waves me over. 'Well, hello there, young lady.' He's not wearing his cap now, and his hair is silver, like his moustache. He sounds posh, I think he's English. Up close, I can see scars on one side of his face. I make sure I don't stare. 'We saw you with a suitcase yesterday, didn't we? Are you on holiday?'

I want to say *Who'd come here on holiday?* but that

would be rude, so I just mutter, 'I'm staying with my aunty and uncle.'

'We're having bara brith,' the nurse says. They're sitting at a table set for morning tea, and all the crockery has *Ynysfach Bowling Club* written on it in red. 'Would you like some? There's plenty.'

'Not if I have anything to do with it,' the man says, grabbing two slices from the biggest plate. 'I like *bara brith*.' He laughs, and his eyes crinkle up.

I giggle. His attempt at a Welsh accent is bad, but funny.

The nurse shakes her head. 'He's a right one, this one.'

I haven't had breakfast, so I sit and take a piece of the fruity loaf. 'Thank you.'

'I'm Lavinia,' the nurse says, pouring tea into cups. 'That's Johnny over there.' The sad soldier stares out over the bowling green, pressing a hand to his jacket pocket. 'And this is Charles, our resident wit. Or so he thinks.' She gives me a wink. 'What's your name?'

'Natty.'

'That's a pretty name. Is that short for Natalie?'

'Yes.'

Lavinia passes me a cup. 'You can join us whenever you're passing,' she says. 'We're here most days.'

'Yes,' Charles says. 'Come and say hello to an old boy and that young scrap.' He points at Johnny.

'Is he all right?' I ask.

'It's the fugue,' Charles says.

'Pardon?'

'Hysterical fugue,' he says. 'Memory loss with no obvious damage to the brain.'

'Oh.'

'He was found wandering around a village in Belgium in civilian clothes. No idea who he was or how he got there,' Lavinia says. 'But he spoke English with a Welsh accent so was shipped back here for treatment.'

'And is it working?' I ask.

She sighs. 'Sometimes we think there's progress, but he still doesn't know who he is. His name's not even Johnny.' She looks at him curiously. 'Well, as far as we know.'

'But the war ended ages ago!'

'It did,' Charles says. 'But we all bring it home. And now it's locked away tight in a little corner of Johnny's mind.' He taps the side of his wheelchair. 'What happened on those battlefields never really leaves us.'

I think of Huw. At the pigsty, fit and strong, whirling Nerys around. Joking in the workshop. Slamming the dresser drawer. The battlefields haven't left him either.

Charles sips his tea. 'Sometimes Johnny remembers little flashes of things.'

'That's good,' I say.

'It depends what he remembers.'

We sit for a while, chatting about nothing in particular. When I've finished my tea and cake, I stand. 'Better go.'

'Come and see us again.' Charles smiles. 'I can show you some magic tricks.'

'He's very good,' Lavinia says proudly.

'I'd like that,' I say, tucking my chair in. 'See you soon.'

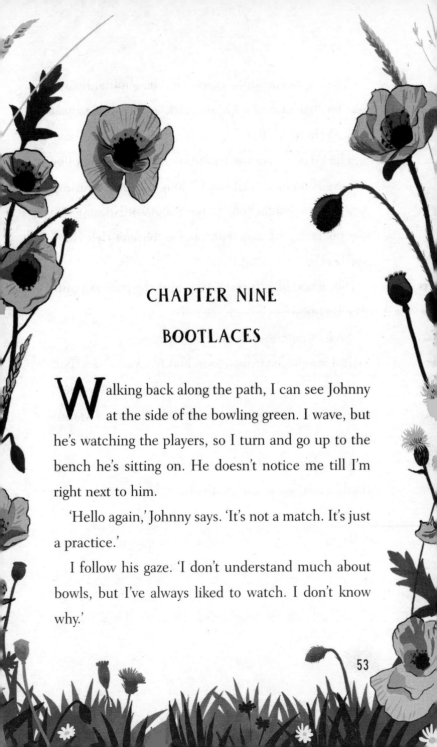

CHAPTER NINE

BOOTLACES

Walking back along the path, I can see Johnny at the side of the bowling green. I wave, but he's watching the players, so I turn and go up to the bench he's sitting on. He doesn't notice me till I'm right next to him.

'Hello again,' Johnny says. 'It's not a match. It's just a practice.'

I follow his gaze. 'I don't understand much about bowls, but I've always liked to watch. I don't know why.'

53

'I like it because it's quiet. No one shouts. It's not like football or rugby. Or even cricket.' He looks up at me. 'Perhaps it's that.'

His Welsh accent is not from round here. Might be west – he sounds a bit like Chippy Gaynor's dad, and he's from Carmarthen. I shove my hands deep into my pockets and watch the bowls run smoothly and softly across the neat lawn.

'Sit, if you like,' he says, watching the players again. 'I don't mind.'

So I sit next to him on the bench.

His hands don't shake now and I'm glad about that. Every now and again, he touches his jacket pocket. It's like he does it without thinking, like a nervous habit or comfort.

Johnny claps along when someone hits the jack. 'Perhaps I used to like football – or rugby – before the war. I can't remember … Did Charles and Lavinia tell you?'

'Yes,' I say. 'But they weren't gossiping.'

'It's all right, I don't mind.'

I think about that word. *Perhaps*. Imagine not

knowing what you liked. 'You might have played bowls,' I say. 'And that's why you like it now.'

Johnny shrugs, looking more like a schoolboy than a soldier. 'They're having speckled bread.' He points to the pavilion.

'*We* say that – me and my mother do!'

'Say what?'

'We call bara brith "speckled bread", like you just did.'

'Did I?' He rubs his forehead and frowns. 'I did, didn't I? But why? No one at Talbot House calls it that. I wonder why that name came into my head just now. I don't understand my own brain. Like, why can I remember how to tie my bootlaces –' he lifts his foot as if to prove he's done it – 'but I can't remember being taught?'

'I don't know.' I wish I did.

'There was another lad in the field hospital who'd lost his memory,' he goes on. 'They sent his family a telegram so they could write him letters, remind him of who he was. Turned out he supported Spurs. I think he was surprised, because he's not even English.'

He laughs. It's very small, but it is a laugh.

'If they could find his family, why can't anyone find yours?' I ask.

'It's not that easy.' Johnny fiddles with the button on his pocket. He's trying to open it. His fingers are shaking again, and I have to really stop myself from offering to help. He manages to get it undone, slips his hand inside and pulls out a bracelet.

It sits in his palm, and now I'm not sure it's a bracelet at all. It's got a chunky chain and a flat, oval, battered metal plate in the middle.

'It's my identity tag,' he says. It jiggles from the shake of his hand. 'See there? The writing?' He tries to point at it, but his finger is shaking too. 'Gah! You hold it.'

I take it from him and read what I can see, which isn't much. It looks like there's meant to be four lines but hardly any letters or numbers are clear. Some parts are smoothed out and the writing has been flattened away, some of it's twisted and scratched. You can tell it's been to war.

'That's supposed to be my name,' he says. 'At the top.'

'They gave us these,' he goes on, 'so if we were injured or killed they'd be able to tell who we were, and let our loved ones know.' He laughs, but it's not in a happy way. 'And here I am, with a battered tag and an empty head, and no way of ever knowing. You've heard people talk – they say things about soldiers coming home from the war, but I didn't come home, did I? I just came –' he waves a hand through the air – '*here*.'

'Your memory might come back,' I say quietly.

'The doctors have tried everything they can think of.' He takes the tag and puts it back in his pocket. He doesn't even try to do up the button. 'Like new it was – the lad in the hospital's tag.'

The bowls click and thud.

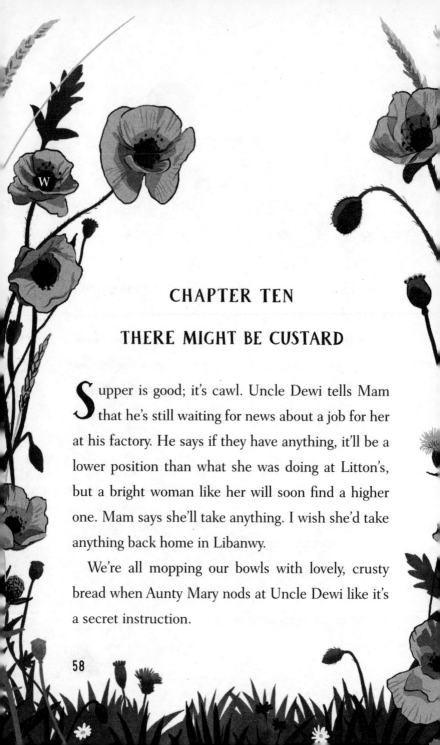

CHAPTER TEN

THERE MIGHT BE CUSTARD

Supper is good; it's cawl. Uncle Dewi tells Mam that he's still waiting for news about a job for her at his factory. He says if they have anything, it'll be a lower position than what she was doing at Litton's, but a bright woman like her will soon find a higher one. Mam says she'll take anything. I wish she'd take anything back home in Libanwy.

We're all mopping our bowls with lovely, crusty bread when Aunty Mary nods at Uncle Dewi like it's a secret instruction.

He clears his throat as if he's trying to sound casual. 'I'm going down the Copper House for a pint after, boy. Said I'd see Ted there. You should come.'

'It might do you good,' Aunty Mary says, a bit too cheerfully. 'You haven't been into the village for such a long time.'

Huw frowns. 'Why? Why would I want to sit in a pub with a minister?'

'Ted's not just a minister. He's a good friend,' Uncle Dewi says. 'And it's only a pint, boy. That's all.'

'It's not though, is it?' Huw puts down his spoon. 'Because Ted will try to get me to go back to chapel – he can't help himself – and I'd rather not listen to how God works in mysterious ways. I've seen how he works and I didn't appreciate it. And I don't appreciate you and Mam cooking things up behind my back either.' Aunty Mary opens her mouth but Huw carries on. 'Don't act so innocent – I saw the way you looked at each other just then.'

'Don't be rude to your mother,' Uncle Dewi says, his voice getting louder.

Huw takes a big breath. 'I'm sorry. I just need you all to stop pushing.'

'I don't push!' Nerys says with a squeak.

'No, little sister, you never do anything wrong, do you?'

She beams, but I'm not sure he meant it that way. For all her books and scholarship talk, she's such a baby sometimes. Uncle Dewi goes into the scullery and turns the tap on hard, the water whooshing into the sink.

I don't like this mood, so pretend I'm too full for afters and go into the yard. The pigs are snuffling around, all wrinkled snouts and floppy ears. I close my eyes and see Johnny's tag in his shaking hand. I was right yesterday when I thought he looked lost, but it isn't in the same way as me at all. As out of place as I feel here, I know who I am. Johnny can't remember. But if he does, he'll know the things he's seen. Like Huw does.

I don't know which is worse.

'Imagine if all you had to worry about was getting fed.' A quiet voice comes from behind me. 'Must be nice.'

I turn to see Huw, smiling in an awkward sort of way. He comes and leans on the fence, next to me. I want to say it isn't nice to be hungry but I know he didn't mean it like that.

'Do you have worries, Natty?' he asks.

What do I say? That I'm worried what my mother will do next? That she'll go through job after job and we'll either have to move again, or she won't get one at all and I'll be stuck sharing a bed with Nerys forever?

But he doesn't seem to mind my silence. He goes on. 'No, the pigs are just happy to eat and eat until they're nice and big and fat. They trust us, you know. They have no idea we feed them and look after them so we can eat them.' He stares into the pen. 'They do what they're supposed to do until they're killed.'

I have a horrible feeling he isn't talking about pigs any more.

'I can't imagine what the war was like.' As soon as I've said it I wish I hadn't, I wish I could take the words and stuff them back in my stupid mouth. They sound so empty and pointless and small.

But Huw smiles. 'No. No, you can't imagine,' he says. 'But at least you realise that.'

I smile back. He scratches the nearest pig's hairy back.

'I thought they weren't dogs,' I say.

He grins. 'Nah, they're all right if you know what you're doing. See? Like this.'

I copy him and the pig snuffles happily.

'Didn't you want any afters?' he asks.

I shake my head.

'Me neither, but it's treacle pudding and Mam does it lovely. I think we might have made a mistake there.' He tilts his head towards the house. 'Go back in? There might be custard.'

I follow him across the yard.

No one's in the kitchen. Huw takes bowls from the dresser and dishes up the pudding. We sit at the table together. He passes me the jug and I pour the custard for both of us.

'It's a bit cold,' he says, moving to get up. 'I can warm it.'

'I like it like this,' I say.

'Tidy.' He takes a big spoonful.

Heavy thuds echo above our heads, we look up at the same time. 'Nerys,' he says. 'For a small person, she doesn't half make a lot of noise.'

'And not just with her feet either.' I screw my face up. I shouldn't have said that. She's his sister. 'Sorry.'

But Huw's laughing. 'Don't worry about it, mun. Chopsiest girl in the valley, our Nerys.'

The thuds get closer. A second later she bursts through the kitchen door. 'Oh,' she says, stopping dead. 'What are you two doing?'

'Having afters,' Huw says, raising his spoon.

'Without me?'

'You've had yours, greedy guts.'

Her eyes move from Huw to me with a look I can't quite work out, then she skips over to the sink. 'Anyway, Aunty Ffion lent me some union newspapers – and a book by Mrs Pankhurst.'

'Did she now?' Huw says. 'And how is old Emmeline?'

'Revolutionary!' Nerys fills a glass with water and

crosses the kitchen, then calls back from the door, 'Just like Aunty Ffion!'

'Marvellous,' I mutter into my bowl. 'Flipping marvellous.'

Because that's all I need – a miniature Mam in my life.

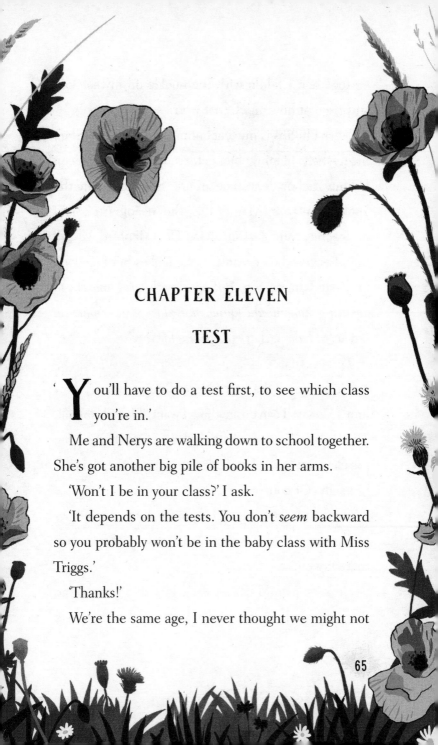

CHAPTER ELEVEN

TEST

'You'll have to do a test first, to see which class you're in.'

Me and Nerys are walking down to school together. She's got another big pile of books in her arms.

'Won't I be in your class?' I ask.

'It depends on the tests. You don't *seem* backward so you probably won't be in the baby class with Miss Triggs.'

'Thanks!'

We're the same age, I never thought we might not

65

be together. I fiddle with the buckle on my satchel, surprised at how much that worries me.

'Miss Phillips is my teacher most of the time. She's nice, she's helping me get ready for the Brecon County School entrance exam.' She holds up the books. 'But Mr Manford is the headmaster, and he teaches some lessons. Mad Dog Manford we call him, because he's dreadful.' She makes her face look mean and angry. '*You, Williams, will never amount to anything. You should know your place, girl. Domestic service or babies, that's the future for you!*'

'He *says* that?'

'He says it all the time.' Nerys shrugs. 'But I'll show him. Dad says I can do anything I want, if I apply myself. That means *do my best with the brains God gave me*. I'm the cleverest in the family, see. And top of the class.'

I sigh. 'Of course you are.'

On the playground, Nerys points to a group of boys playing tag. 'That one there,' she says, 'the lanky one, that's Owen.'

He sees us and comes over. His skin is pale and there are dark circles under his eyes, but he's very

66

smiley. 'You must be Natty. Nerys didn't stop talking about you yesterday.'

She nods. 'That's true, I didn't.'

When he reaches up to straighten his cap, I notice a long red welt across his palm. Nerys must do too because she takes his wrist and has a closer look. 'My mam's got some ointment that'll help with that.'

Owen pulls his hand away. 'It'll go. At least it was only one stroke.' He pushes his hands deep in his pockets. 'Albert got six of the best.'

'I did!' Another boy, stocky and fair-haired, races past us. He laughs and slaps Owen hard on the back. 'Tag! You're it!'

Owen chases after him.

'*That's* Albert Sullivan,' Nerys says heavily. '*He's* an idiot.'

Nerys takes me straight to the secretary's office. 'You're doing your test in here,' she says, tapping on the door. A stiff-looking woman in a high-collared dress opens it. 'Good morning, Miss Nicol,' Nerys says. 'This is my cousin, Natalie Lydiate.'

Miss Nicol nods. 'Yes, yes, I am almost ready. You may come in, Natalie.'

'Please, miss,' I say. 'I like to be called Natty.'

It's as if I said something awful. 'And *I* like little girls who don't tell me what to do, *Natalie*.' She looks at Nerys. 'Off you go then. Unless you're sitting the test too?'

'I wish I was,' Nerys says. 'I love tests, but I have a job to do for Miss Phillips. I don't know what it is, but I expect it's something important. Perhaps I'll be the new pencil monitor. May Morgan's not very good at sharpening. Miss Phillips says there'll be no pencils left if—'

'Nerys Williams!' Miss Nicol holds a hand in the air. '*I said*, off you go.'

Nerys twirls the ends of her hair. 'Yes, miss. Sorry, miss.' Then smiles at me and mouths, *Good luck*.

In the small office, Miss Nicol points to a desk in the corner. On it is a booklet and a pen. She fills the inkpot while I sit. 'You have as much time as you need to complete the test,' she says, screwing the top back on the ink jar. 'Begin when you are ready.'

I flick through the booklet. Grammar, arithmetic and a page of questions about a poem – it doesn't look too difficult. I think I'll escape the 'baby class'.

I can't do all the sums, but I try my best and the grammar is easy enough. I've always been quite good at that. The poem is one I've seen before, one about the war;

'Strange Hells' by Ivor Gurney. It begins:

There are strange Hells within the minds War made

and I think of Huw and Johnny, and if there's hell inside their minds. It's quite hard to concentrate after that.

It's just after eleven o'clock when I put down my pen and tell Miss Nicol I've finished.

'Leave everything on the desk. You're free to go now.' She carries on typing.

But I don't know where I'm supposed to go. I stand and do a little cough. She looks up. 'Why are you still here?'

I tug at the hem of my sleeve. 'Erm … please can you tell me where my classroom is, Miss Nicol?'

'No one will know the answer to that until Miss Phillips has assessed your abilities, Natalie.' She walks across the room, picks up the booklet and flicks through it. I wish she wouldn't. 'And you'll find out when you come to school with your cousin in the morning. For now, you are to go home.'

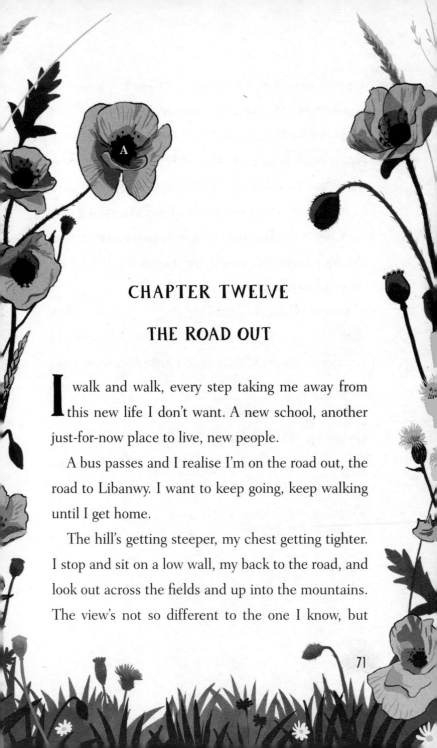

CHAPTER TWELVE

THE ROAD OUT

I walk and walk, every step taking me away from this new life I don't want. A new school, another just-for-now place to live, new people.

A bus passes and I realise I'm on the road out, the road to Libanwy. I want to keep going, keep walking until I get home.

The hill's getting steeper, my chest getting tighter. I stop and sit on a low wall, my back to the road, and look out across the fields and up into the mountains. The view's not so different to the one I know, but

I might as well be a hundred miles away.

There's the Gweld, and the open space Nerys said is good for picnics and rolling down. An odd, spluttering laugh bursts out of me as I picture her tumbling down the mountain. I bet she goes like heck.

Now that I've caught my breath, I get up and step over the wall. The road to Libanwy disappears over the top of the hill. Grudgingly I turn and head back down to Ynysfach.

In the distance, between the trees and yellow daffodils, is a perfect square. The bowling green. I wonder if Johnny, Charles and Lavinia are there now. She said they are most days.

I smile, remembering Charles's jokes and Johnny saying 'speckled bread'. It felt like – I don't know – like we had something in common. More than me and Nerys ever will. Maybe because this is her home, not ours. Me, Johnny, Charles … we've all been forced to come here, we didn't choose this place. I look down at my boots as I walk, at my bootlaces, and Johnny's words float into my mind:

But I didn't come home, did I?

All that time in Belgium, when all they ever wanted was to win the war and get back home. That's so much worse than Mam losing another job and us having to come to Ynysfach. Here I am, feeling sorry for myself, when Johnny doesn't even know where his home is.

A mad thought comes into my head.

And it grows and grows.

I walk faster, towards the park.

Through the gates, up the slope, turning right, I'm just heading to the pavilion when a voice calls from behind me. I spin round to see Johnny coming along the path.

Perfect timing.

'Just been for a walk,' he says, catching up. 'I don't feel like sitting around today. Charles and Lavinia are at the pavilion though, if you want to see them.'

'I came to see you, actually,' I say.

'Me?'

'Yes … I want to ask you something. Something important. And it's all right if you don't want to answer. I just … well …'

One corner of his mouth goes up. 'Go on.'

We start walking together, back along the path away from the bowling green.

'It's about bara brith.'

'Oh, cake, yes – very important.'

'I mean, about how you called it speckled bread.'

Johnny frowns, his shaking hand going to his jacket pocket, fiddling with the button. 'What about it?'

I'm suddenly afraid that I might ruin our friendship before it's really begun. But I can't stop now. 'I want to help you.'

'Help me do what?'

'I've been thinking.' I look at the path, the flowers, anywhere but at him. 'Perhaps it's the small things that will help you remember who you are. The things from before you were a soldier. "Speckled bread" is usually what little children say.'

Johnny's got a faraway look in his eyes. We keep walking, and the silence is awful, and everything I'd thought of when I was walking down the hill is going to sound stupid out loud. But I have to say it.

'You said the doctors have tried everything they can

think of. But what if *I* can think of something else? Because Huw – that's my cousin – he went to war too, and he brought it home, like Charles said. In his head, I mean. But Huw paints, and he feels happier then, when he's not really thinking at all. So maybe that's what you need, to stop *trying* to remember. We could play a game – or draw a picture – if you like.' I scrunch up my face and look at him in a hopeful way.

'You want to play a game?'

'Yes,' I say, feeling like a bit of an idiot. 'Anything, really. Then the memories might come by themselves.'

Johnny stares down the path, squinting slightly in the sunshine. 'Perhaps,' he says.

That word again.

Perhaps.

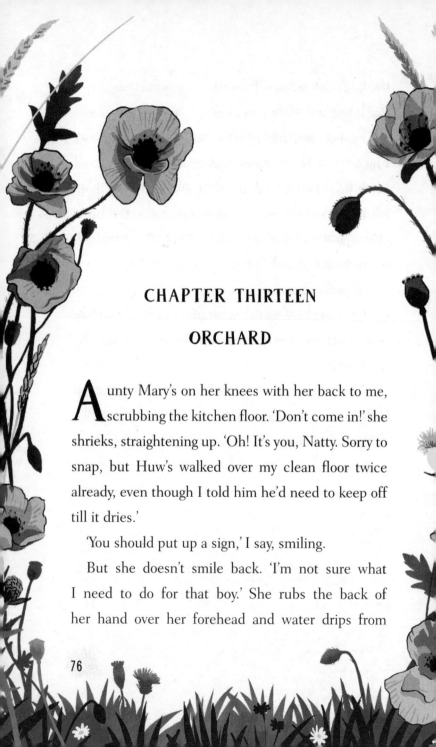

CHAPTER THIRTEEN

ORCHARD

Aunty Mary's on her knees with her back to me, scrubbing the kitchen floor. 'Don't come in!' she shrieks, straightening up. 'Oh! It's you, Natty. Sorry to snap, but Huw's walked over my clean floor twice already, even though I told him he'd need to keep off till it dries.'

'You should put up a sign,' I say, smiling.

But she doesn't smile back. 'I'm not sure what I need to do for that boy.' She rubs the back of her hand over her forehead and water drips from

76

the brush on to her headscarf.

'I'll stay out of the way,' I say.

'You can help your mam in the orchard,' Aunty Mary says. 'She's looking for gaps in the hedge. I think it's another way that daft puppy is getting in. Found him in the scullery with his snout in the veg basket earlier, I did! Trailed muck everywhere!' She waves a hand at the floor.

'All right, I'll go up there then.'

Huw's in his workshop, frowning over his sketch-book. He doesn't see me wave as I pass.

Through the arched gate, a small field slopes upwards, with trees set out in lines and rows. The tall hedge is all around, like a green wall. I walk past apple trees and pear trees but can't see Mam. Right up at the far end, where there are plums, I find her. She's twtying down, with her hands in the bottom of the hedge.

She hears me coming and turns. 'Oh, hello, love.'

'Aunty Mary said you were here. Is that where he's getting in?' I ask. 'The farmer's pup?'

She frowns and turns back to the hedge. 'I think it

could be,' she says, her voice slightly muffled as she sticks her head inside. 'But it's going to be tricky to keep him out. He's so small he can wriggle through most gaps.' She pops her head back out and grins at me. 'And he can dig!'

She sits on the grass and taps the ground next to her. 'How was school? Not finished already, is it?'

'I had to do tests and then leave,' I say, sitting down. 'The secretary said they'll know by tomorrow which class I can go in.'

'And how were the tests?'

I shrug. 'Fine.'

'That's my girl.' She puts her arm around me and kisses the top of my head. 'It will be all right, you know. Being here. It will all work out.'

I resist the urge to answer with *That's what you always say* because I don't want to spoil this. It's nice, sitting here in the orchard with Mam.

CHAPTER FOURTEEN

YSGOL YNYSFACH

I'm in the same class as Nerys.

A tall man in a long, black gown paces in front of the blackboard, staring at the floor, his hands behind his back. Above him is a sign which reads:

> *Foolishness is bound in the heart of*
> *a child;*
> *but the rod of correction shall drive it far*
> *from him.*
> *Proverbs 22:15*

Flipping heck. I know what that means – any messing around and we'll get the cane. Like Owen and Albert.

I sit at the end of the first row of desks. There are four rows altogether, each one fixed on a step so we slope upwards like we're in a very small theatre. There's even a gap in the middle like an aisle. The desks are long, and fit three children on each. I'm next to a sour-faced girl who keeps elbowing me when she writes on her slate. Nerys is at the back and smiles whenever I dare turn around to try to see a friendly face. I'm glad she's there. A tall girl with plaits is standing, reciting her seven times table.

When she finishes, Mr Manford nods. 'All correct, Ivy. A significant improvement on your last effort. You may sit.'

Ivy sits.

Mr Manford points at Owen, who stands. He's at the other end of my row but, even from here, I can see he's trembling.

'Begin,' Mr Manford says.

Owen does as he's told. 'One seven is seven,

two sevens are fourteen.' He stops, blinks, goes to say 'three' but Mr Manford holds up a hand.

'There'll be no pausing to work it out. From the beginning, boy.'

Owen starts again, and gets further. 'Six times seven is forty-nine … no … erm …' I watch him, willing him on, hoping he gets to the end without too much trouble. Two boys snigger behind him; one of them is Albert Sullivan. Nerys glares at them.

'Master Elias,' Mr Manford says, slowly, like he's speaking to someone really stupid. 'If you cannot recite your seven times table, you must be either lazy or a dunce. Neither is tolerated in this class. *Again.*'

'Mr Manford won't let him sit down until he gets them all right,' the girl next to me whispers, looking delighted.

Nasty little madam.

Nerys leans forward in her seat, staring at Owen so hard I think she's trying to send the right answers into his head. But it's no use, he's coming apart. Starting over and over again until he can't even get past two times seven. Owen blinks again, many times. I'm sure he's trying not to cry.

'Shall we see if Miss Triggs has room in her class, Master Elias?' Mr Manford asks.

The girl next to me snorts with laughter. Owen's skinny chest is heaving, his hands scrunch into fists, he swipes an arm across his desk. His slate clatters to the floor.

'HOW *DARE* YOU?' Mr Manford thunders, so loud we all jump in our seats. 'COME HERE, BOY!'

Owen, red-faced and shaking, moves slowly along the row, down the step and across the floor.

'Hand,' Mr Manford commands. Owen holds out his right hand. 'The *other* one.'

Oh no, not his sore hand.

Owen opens his left palm and looks into his headteacher's face.

'Seven, I think,' Mr Manford says. 'To remind you to learn your tables.'

By the last stroke of the cane, Owen is shaking like heck, but he never stops looking at Mr Manford.

Never shows how much it hurts. When it's over, before Mr Manford can say anything else, Owen crosses the room and picks up a pointed hat from a stool in the corner and sits facing the wall.

I risk a glance at Nerys. She's wiping away tears.

The nasty sour-faced girl is next. May Morgan, Mr Manford calls her. She only reaches halfway and gets most of those wrong. Good – let's see how she likes a dose of Mad Dog Manford's rage. She deserves it after laughing at Owen.

But he tells her to sit back down.

I can't believe it. That's the most unfair thing I've ever seen!

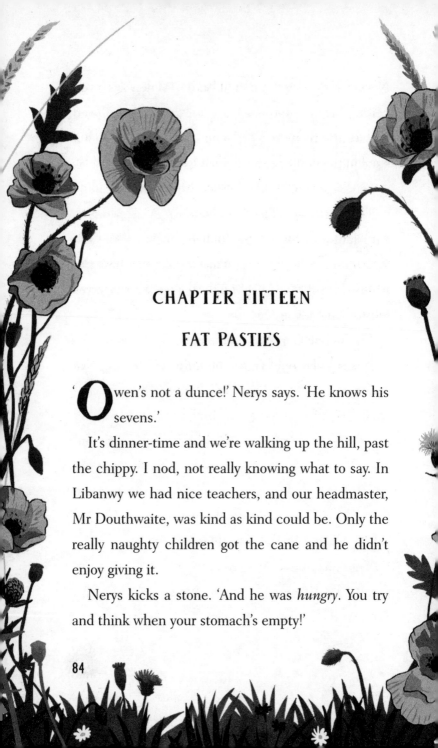

CHAPTER FIFTEEN

FAT PASTIES

'Owen's not a dunce!' Nerys says. 'He knows his sevens.'

It's dinner-time and we're walking up the hill, past the chippy. I nod, not really knowing what to say. In Libanwy we had nice teachers, and our headmaster, Mr Douthwaite, was kind as kind could be. Only the really naughty children got the cane and he didn't enjoy giving it.

Nerys kicks a stone. 'And he was *hungry*. You try and think when your stomach's empty!'

'I wish he'd come to Fferm Fach with us for dinner,' I say.

'Too proud. You saw how he looked at Mad Dog when he took his lashes. I wish he wouldn't – it just makes Mad Dog hit him harder.' She suddenly splutters and tears roll down her cheeks.

Owen *is* proud. Even though Nerys offered to share her milk at playtime, because he didn't have the penny it costs to buy his own, he'd looked sideways at me and said no.

'Can't Owen's parents complain? Mam would.'

Nerys looks right at me and almost laughs. 'Not everyone has a mam like yours, Natty.' She sniffs, and wipes her face with the back of her hand. 'Owen's mam and dad are just grateful he has an education. They haven't got a say in how he gets it. The poor children get picked on the most, and Owen more than anyone else, because he won't cry. Mad Dog wants to break him like a wild pony.'

'That's heartless.'

'Oh, Mad Dog has a heart,' Nerys says. 'And it's black as the coal they dig out in Llanbryn.'

Uncle Dewi's home for his dinner. He's outside the back door, sitting at a table set with fat pasties, a bottle of pop and a small jug of flowers. Aunty Mary comes out with some plates. She nods at the jug. 'Your mam's idea,' she says. 'Oh! Nerys, what's the matter, love?'

Nerys's lip wobbles and she flings herself into her mother's pinny. Aunty Mary looks at me.

'Mad Dog ...' I say. 'I mean Mr Manford ... he was really, really horrible to Owen.'

'Not again!' Aunty Mary sits Nerys on a chair and pours her some lemonade. Uncle Dewi shakes his head slowly.

'It was worse this time, Mam,' Nerys mumbles. 'He got the cane *and* the dunce's cap.'

'It was *awful*,' I say. 'I didn't know anyone could be so cruel.'

Aunty Mary gives my shoulder a little squeeze as she sits down.

Mam appears in the doorway, wiping her hands on a tea towel. 'Sounds like someone needs to stand up to this Mr Manford.'

'What do you mean?' Nerys asks.

But I know what she means, and my stomach sinks at the thought. Because this is always the way it starts, with Mam wanting to fix a problem that isn't hers to fix.

'I mean he can't be allowed to get away with it.' She sits down. 'Tell me everything.'

Aunty Mary's watching Mam, and I wonder if she's thinking the same as me. Ffion Lydiate – Champion of the Underdog – is about to stir up trouble. And this time in Ynysfach. Nerys tells them what happened this morning and the more Mam hears, the more spirited she gets.

And Uncle Dewi's the same. 'Manford's only interested in families who have standing in the community.'

'Like May Morgan,' Nerys says. 'She's a councillor's daughter, so can do no wrong.'

May Morgan; she was the one sat next to me. No wonder nothing happened when she made mistakes.

Uncle Dewi nods. 'But if your father gets his hands dirty or your mother takes in washing, well, you're just low-born and ought to know your place. But you know how the world works, Ffion, you don't have to be a child to be put upon by the likes of *Mister* Manford. If you don't move in their circles, they have the power.'

Nerys throws her hands up. 'And there's nothing we can do.'

'There's always something we can do,' Mam says.

I knew it. She wants to help. Doesn't she realise her way of 'helping' is what landed us here in the first place? Owen's got parents, let them complain.

I take a pasty and bite into it. It's lovely; still warm and full of corned beef, potatoes and carrots. I think of Owen and the other children, and what they'll be having. If anything. And I wish I could help, I really do. But Mam's way will only make things worse.

'I've worked for a few tyrants,' Mam says. 'And they don't like it when we stand up to them.'

'So what would *you* do,' Nerys asks, 'if it was in your factory?'

Oh, Nerys, why did you have to go and ask?

'There are various ways,' Mam says. 'Keeping records, lodging a grievance, go-slows.'

'The children don't know what you mean, Ffion,' Aunty Mary says, flicking a crumb off the tablecloth.

'Writing things down, complaining, working slow on purpose.'

From the look on Aunty Mary's face I don't think she'd wanted Mam to explain.

'That's all very well,' Uncle Dewi says. 'But those sorts of things won't work in a school.'

Nerys does a huge, exaggerated sigh and flops over the table. 'It's just not fair.'

'Life isn't.' I drink my pop.

'I'm going for a walk around the orchard,' Nerys says, grabbing her pasty and dragging her feet miserably across the yard.

'See, Mam?' I say. 'There isn't *always something we can do*.'

She does that face where her lips go tight to stop herself from arguing.

Aunty Mary stands, smooths her pinny and goes off to see Huw in his workshop. Five minutes later,

Nerys streaks back across the yard, the straps of her apron flying behind her.

'I've got it!' she yells, running past us and into the house. 'I know what we can do!'

Then she's back, waving what look like thin magazines in the air. We all stare at her. She puts her hands on her hips and pants dramatically.

'Dad, you said the sorts of things Aunty Ffion talked about won't work in a school.'

'Yes,' Uncle Dewi says slowly.

'So we don't do anything *in* school. We stay out of it.' She's looking at us like she expects us to know what she's on about.

We don't.

She grins. 'We call a strike!'

She's gone mad.

'Children can't go on strike,' I say.

'Oh, but they can!' Nerys says. 'It's been done before. It's all in the union newspapers that your mam gave me. I'll show you.'

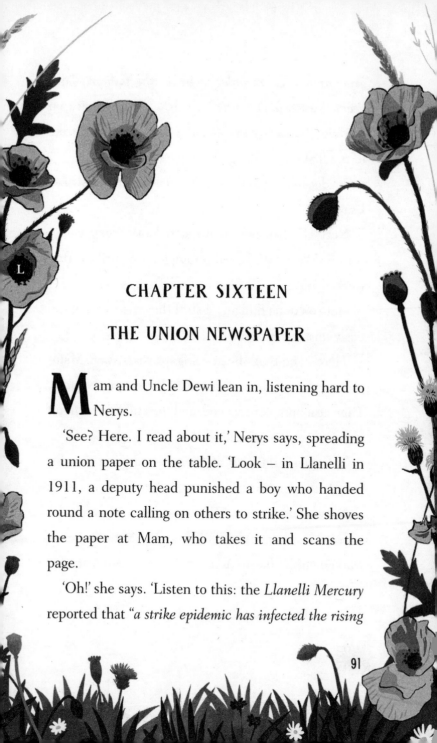

CHAPTER SIXTEEN

THE UNION NEWSPAPER

Mam and Uncle Dewi lean in, listening hard to Nerys.

'See? Here. I read about it,' Nerys says, spreading a union paper on the table. 'Look – in Llanelli in 1911, a deputy head punished a boy who handed round a note calling on others to strike.' She shoves the paper at Mam, who takes it and scans the page.

'Oh!' she says. 'Listen to this: the *Llanelli Mercury* reported that "*a strike epidemic has infected the rising generation who, in order to be 'in the fashion', have decided upon a 'down-tool' policy"* …' She carries on reading. 'It doesn't say why the boy wanted to strike in the first place though.'

'It doesn't sound like they even had a strike,' I say.

Nerys flashes me an irritated look. 'Keep going, Aunty Ffion. We need examples of strikes that worked.'

'Bet you don't find any.' I stuff the crusty end of the pasty into my mouth.

'Here's one that's been going for years,' says Mam, glancing at me, 'in a place called Burston in Norfolk. Their teachers were sacked, and the children went on strike to get them back.'

'Imagine if the girls at Litton's had done that for you,' I say.

Nerys scowls at me. 'That's not very nice, Natty.'

I ignore her. 'And this one in Norfolk hasn't worked either, has it? You just said it's been going for years.'

'No, but the whole community backed them – they

even raised money to build a new school where their teachers could work. So it's making a difference.'

Nerys blows out a long breath. 'That's good, but we don't want to *keep* Mr Manford. In fact, I'd much rather we got rid of him. Could we strike for that?'

'Hmm, probably not,' Uncle Dewi says. 'Too much power and influence supporting him. Plus, it's not against the law for teachers to hit children.'

I'm getting really fed up of this now and I want them to stop. I put my glass of pop down. 'You're going about this the wrong way.'

Mam and Nerys share a baffled look.

'Go on,' Uncle Dewi says.

'You write to the council and ask for free school dinners. See? Simple. No need to make a fuss.'

'What do you mean?' Mam asks.

'Owen was punished for getting things wrong, but he was hungry. You said it yourself, Nerys – *You try and think when your stomach's empty.* It's not a strike they need, it's food.'

'No,' Mam says quietly, a grin spreading across her

face. 'It's both. If the council were going to give you free school dinners, they'd have done it by now. You need to shock them into it. You strike for food!'

'Yes! Free dinners, like in Libanwy!' Nerys leaps up, then frowns and sits back down. 'Oh.'

'What's wrong, love?' Uncle Dewi asks.

'It's just … well …' she says. 'We can't make Owen the centre of it.'

Good, that's the end of the whole stupid strike idea then.

'Ah, but we don't have to, do we?' Mam's on her feet now, flitting about like one of chickens. 'He isn't the only hungry one.'

Nerys bounces excitedly in her seat. 'All right then. We'll do it. We'll strike for food!'

Oh no.

'Wonderful idea, Natty!' Uncle Dewi beams. 'Looks like Nerys isn't the only scholar round here.'

'Me? I didn't … I only meant …'

But it's no use.

Nerys squeezes me tight. 'Oh, I'm so glad you came here, Natty.'

94

I peel her off and stand up. 'I'm going back to school.' I grab my satchel and glare at Mam, hoping it might make her remember to ask me how my first morning went. But she's looking at the union newspaper again.

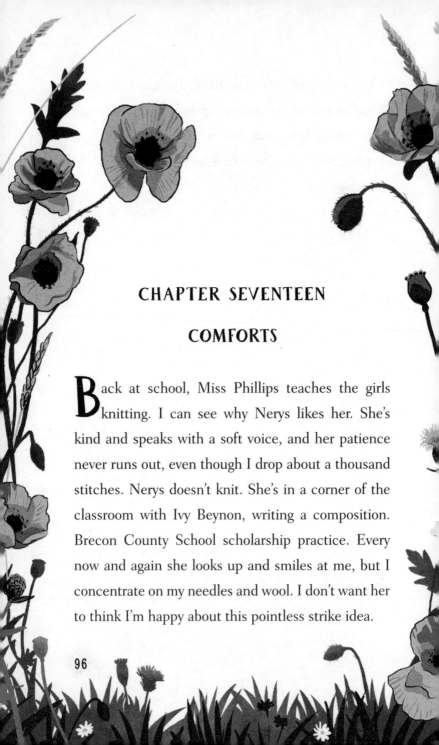

CHAPTER SEVENTEEN

COMFORTS

Back at school, Miss Phillips teaches the girls knitting. I can see why Nerys likes her. She's kind and speaks with a soft voice, and her patience never runs out, even though I drop about a thousand stitches. Nerys doesn't knit. She's in a corner of the classroom with Ivy Beynon, writing a composition. Brecon County School scholarship practice. Every now and again she looks up and smiles at me, but I concentrate on my needles and wool. I don't want her to think I'm happy about this pointless strike idea.

We have singing before home time, led by Mad Dog, but we all belt out the hymns so even he can't find a reason to cane anyone. It's a nice afternoon, which makes it pass quickly.

At the gates, May Morgan – the councillor's sour-faced daughter – pushes past us. She's wearing a bobbly knitted hat, a bit like the kind Scottish people wear in story books. But this one's dark green and makes her head look like a savoy cabbage.

'Watch it!' Owen says.

May gives him what she clearly thinks is a withering glare, but, really, she just looks a bit twp. Then off she goes down the road, her cabbage hat getting smaller and smaller in the distance.

'Don't go home yet,' Nerys says to Owen in a low voice. 'We've had an idea.'

'You're always having ideas.' He looks to me. 'You the same, are you?'

'Nothing to do with me.'

'Oh, pay no attention to her,' Nerys says. 'She's just being a grump.'

Owen eyes us both.

'I'm going.' I walk backwards down the high street. 'I've got better things to do.'

'But we found examples of you-know-whats that worked!' she calls.

I stop, hold my hands up in the air and pull a face to show I don't care, then I turn and stamp off towards the park.

Johnny, Charles and Lavinia are at the pavilion. It's nice to see their friendly faces.

'Well, if it isn't Natty!' Charles beams, putting playing cards into a pack.

'Have you been practising your magic tricks?' I ask.

'You remembered! How kind of you. I said Natty's a good sort, didn't I, Nursey?'

Lavinia smiles. 'No time for magic lessons now though. We're due back for tea very soon.'

'Steak and kidney pie,' Johnny says. He looks different today. Brighter. But then he leans towards me and frowns. 'You all right?'

I sigh. 'Not really. It's … Oh, it doesn't matter. You'll be late for your tea.'

Johnny pulls out the chair next to him. 'We've got time.'

I glance at Lavinia, who gives a little nod, so I sit. It all comes out in a rush – Mad Dog, Owen, Mam and Nerys's strike. Not wanting to be here at all. When I've finished they all look at each other in a concerned sort of way.

'That's a lot for a first day at a new school,' Johnny says.

I look down at my satchel, fiddling with the ends of my knitting needles, feeling silly that I said all that to people I hardly know.

It's like Johnny can tell what's in my head, because he points at the needles to change the subject. 'What are you making?'

'I'm not sure yet.' I show them the red, raggedy thing hanging from one needle. 'It's a bit messy. I'm just practising rows of a new stitch. Might be a scarf. Probably. Scarves are easiest.'

'A lady from the Huddersfield Red Cross knitted

me a scarf as one of my Comforts,' Charles says. 'The kindness of some people! I've never even been to Huddersfield!'

'Comforts?' I ask.

'Knitted joy!' Charles says. 'Gloves, balaclavas and so on, knitted by civilians and sent to us in the trenches. Damned cold it was there …' Lavinia gives him a stern look. 'Oh, pardon my language. *Jolly* cold it was.' He winks at me.

'Socks were the best,' Johnny says.

Charles sits up very straight. 'What?'

'Socks,' Johnny says again. 'Our feet got so wet and cold. Socks were what we all wanted.'

Charles and Lavinia are eyeing Johnny with a look of wonder and worry all mixed together.

'Yes, boy,' Charles says in a voice so soft it doesn't sound like his. 'We wanted socks.' He blinks and, for a second, I think he might cry. Johnny only stares across the park.

'You remembered,' I say. 'You knew socks were the best.'

'Well, erm …' Lavinia says. 'I'm sorry, Natty, but

Johnny might not have *remembered* it as such. He could have heard someone else say it. At Talbot House.'

'Oh.' I hadn't thought of that.

Lavinia puts the pack of cards in her handbag. 'We really need to be going.'

I watch Johnny. It's like the brightness has gone out of him again. He frowns, his hand pressed tight to his jacket pocket.

Charles takes a deep breath and claps Johnny on the back. 'Steak and kidney pie, eh? The food of kings!'

'Natty had an idea,' Johnny says quickly. He looks at me. 'I've been thinking about it.'

My stomach scrunches – what's he going to say?

'And,' he says. 'I know you're not going to like it, Lavinia, but please – hear me out.'

'This doesn't bode well.' She folds her arms. 'Go on.'

'Natty's going to try to help me get my memories back.'

I gasp. 'Really? Oh that's—'

Lavinia's voice goes a bit high. 'What on earth do you mean?'

I pick at the hem of my dress so I don't have to look at her.

'Just that,' Johnny says. 'I feel better talking to her than anyone. It's Natty who helps me remember things, not the doctors.' He smiles at me. 'Like speckled bread.'

I smile back.

'Speckled bread?' Lavinia says. 'What *are* you talking about? And, Natty, I know you mean well, but I don't think this is a good idea. Johnny's mind is very fragile. The doctors have tried all sorts of carefully planned treatments. If—'

'And where has that got him?' Charles asks. 'I don't mean to be rude, Lavinia, but he's hardly better now than when he came back from Belgium. Let the girl try.'

Johnny nods. 'It's my mind – fragile or not – and it's made up. I want Natty to help.'

Lavinia sighs. 'What do you have in mind, Natty?'

Suddenly, saying it to a nurse feels a bit silly, but it helps to see Johnny smiling at me. 'Well,' I say, 'because Johnny remembers little flashes of things, like Charles said –' Charles gives me an encouraging nod – 'I've thought about what might spark a nice memory. What might have been important to him when he was my age – toys, sweets, playing with friends. Nicer things than the war.'

'Go on.'

I look around at them all, desperately hoping they don't think I'm being ridiculous as I tell them about Huw and his workshop and how it helps him. When I finish, Charles is beaming.

'Marvellous idea!'

Lavinia unfolds her arms. 'Well, I suppose it can't do any harm. But any sign of distress – anything at all – you'll stop. I want your word. Both of you.'

'Scout's honour.' Johnny smiles; a proper, eyes-shining smile.

I walk back to Fferm Fach feeling really good for the first time in a week. Johnny wants me to help him. I can *do* something, be useful.

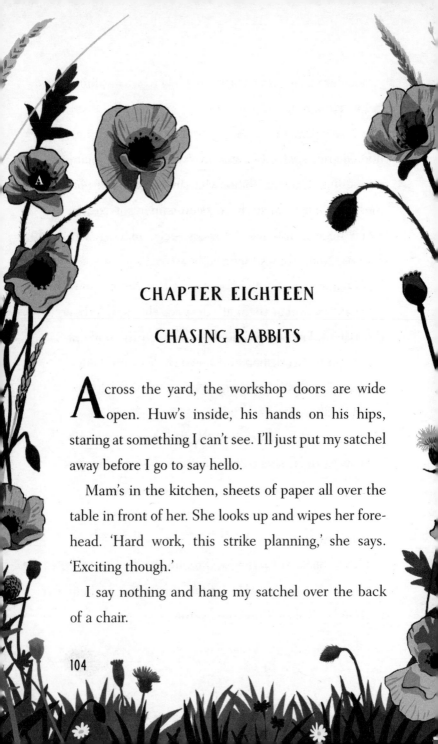

CHAPTER EIGHTEEN

CHASING RABBITS

Across the yard, the workshop doors are wide open. Huw's inside, his hands on his hips, staring at something I can't see. I'll just put my satchel away before I go to say hello.

Mam's in the kitchen, sheets of paper all over the table in front of her. She looks up and wipes her forehead. 'Hard work, this strike planning,' she says. 'Exciting though.'

I say nothing and hang my satchel over the back of a chair.

She does an awkward little cough. 'How was school this afternoon?'

Oh, now she's interested.

'No one got the cane, if that's what you're wondering.' I wave my hand at the papers. 'So you can't add *that* to your list of grievances, or whatever that is.'

'Natty, that wasn't why I was asking.' She gets up. 'Let's have a cup of tea. You can tell me about your whole day.'

I glare at her. 'I don't know what's worse – when you forget to care, or when you pretend to.'

She gasps. I walk out. That's my good mood spoilt.

I breathe deeply as I go across to the workshop. Even strangers I met in the park care more about me than my own mother! They noticed, listened – why can't she be like that?

Huw's standing in front of a canvas. He turns when I get to the door.

'Hello,' he says. 'How was your first day?'

It's all I can do not to burst into tears.

There's a funny little moan from the corner. Sid

Davey's puppy is curled up on a pile of old sheets, fast asleep and twitching. 'Chasing rabbits,' Huw says, smiling.

I go and twty down next to the pup. He wriggles when I stroke his soft fur, but doesn't wake up. The feeling that I need to cry goes away.

Huw comes over and kneels next to me. 'Life of Riley, he's got.'

'All right for some.' The puppy licks my hand. 'What's his name?'

'No idea,' Huw says. 'School not good then?'

'Not this morning, no.' I find that extra-soft spot behind the puppy's ears.

'Ah,' Huw says, sitting back on his heels. 'Mad Dog. I heard about the strike.'

'It's such a stupid idea! It'll all go horribly wrong and it'll be Mam's fault. Again. Putting her grand ideas into Nerys's head.'

'Oh, I don't know – Nerys has a fair few grand ideas of her own.' Huw watches me for a second. 'You're not much like your mother, are you?'

'No. I'm not.'

'I like Aunty Ffion, but she's crackers, mun. Children can't fight teachers and the council! And Nerys – well, she's Nerys. Once she's wound up she goes off like a spinning top.'

I like this. Having Huw on my side. Someone in Fferm Fach who doesn't think Mam is wonderful.

'It's not that I don't care about Owen and the others being hungry, I do care. It's just …'

Huw looks right at me. 'You didn't want to come here, did you?'

'No.' I sigh. 'I didn't. I mean it's nice and everything – and you're all lovely and kind – but we've only been here a few days, and already my flipping mother's going to make us look like troublemakers.'

'It's all right, I'd be the same.'

'We've been forced to move before,' I say, sitting properly now. 'We had some rooms in a woman's house, but Mam and her argued over suffrage and she threw us out. We had to live in a horrible flat till we found our last one. That one was nice. Nicest place we'd been in.'

He puts a hand on my arm, gives it a quick squeeze,

107

then stands. 'Come and have a look at this. I'm trying to get the background right.'

It's the painting he was working on the other day; the two pigs in their sty. He picks up a notebook. 'I did this, but I can't seem to translate it to the canvas.'

It's a pencil sketch of the same picture.

'That's incredible!' I say. Because it is. I've never seen a drawing so good.

He laughs and shrugs. I flick through the book. It's all things from around here. Trees on the Gweld, the animals, the house, the orchard. All close to home, all beautiful.

Huw puts the sketchbook down and passes me a handful of brushes. 'Want to make yourself useful? Find a pot for these.'

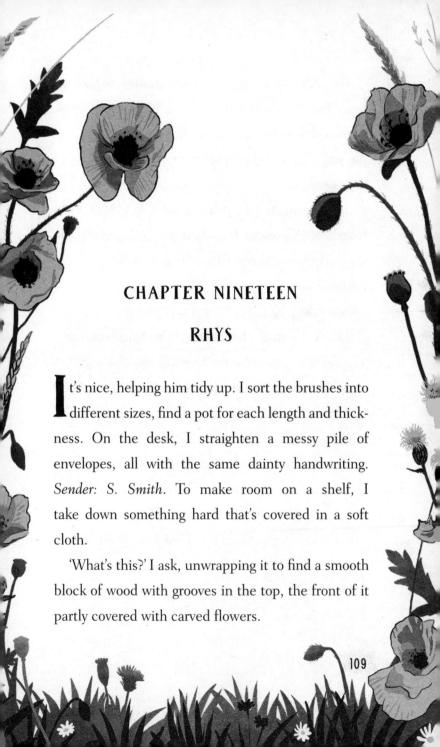

CHAPTER NINETEEN

RHYS

It's nice, helping him tidy up. I sort the brushes into different sizes, find a pot for each length and thickness. On the desk, I straighten a messy pile of envelopes, all with the same dainty handwriting. *Sender: S. Smith.* To make room on a shelf, I take down something hard that's covered in a soft cloth.

'What's this?' I ask, unwrapping it to find a smooth block of wood with grooves in the top, the front of it partly covered with carved flowers.

He turns and an odd look flashes across his face. For a second I think it's going to be like the dresser drawer all over again, but he says, 'It's … it's nothing … just something I never finished.'

'It's lovely.'

'It was going to be a pen rest for Nerys.' He takes it from me. 'A present for when she gets her scholarship. There's a space there, in the middle, for her initials.'

'She'll love it,' I say. 'Why didn't you finish it?'

'I can't.' He runs a hand through his hair. 'Someone – a friend – was showing me how to carve this part. See here?' He points at a swirling stem. 'And I don't know how to do it without him.'

'Why can't he help you now?'

'It was something we started together. In Belgium.'

'Oh.' He means in the war. I search for something to say. 'I'd like to do woodwork, but it's only for boys. Mam said I ought to do it if I want to, make a fuss. But I don't really mind sewing and knitting instead.'

Huw nods, but I don't feel he's listening. He runs a paint-spattered finger over the swirling stem. 'The trenches isn't all bombardment, you know. There's days and days sometimes with nothing to do but count the rats. And you get time off, let some other poor sod take his turn at being cannon fodder. We could go into the villages sometimes. The local people were kind, some boys even found sweethearts there. But most days we had to sit and wait, right near the action, or even in the trenches. Those were the times when me and Rhys – that was my friend – used to write letters or play cards or make things like this.'

'Did Rhys die?' I ask.

Huw laughs in an empty sort of way. 'That's what I like about you, Natty – you ask a straight question. Yeah, Rhys has gone. Best friend I'll ever have.'

'That's …' But what is it? Sad? A shame? Terrible? No words are big enough. Because what do you say when someone tells you their best friend is gone?

He wraps the pen rest in the cloth and puts it back on the shelf. 'Time I got that daft pup home.'

Soon we're walking across the yard, the light from the kitchen deep pink and warm through the flowered

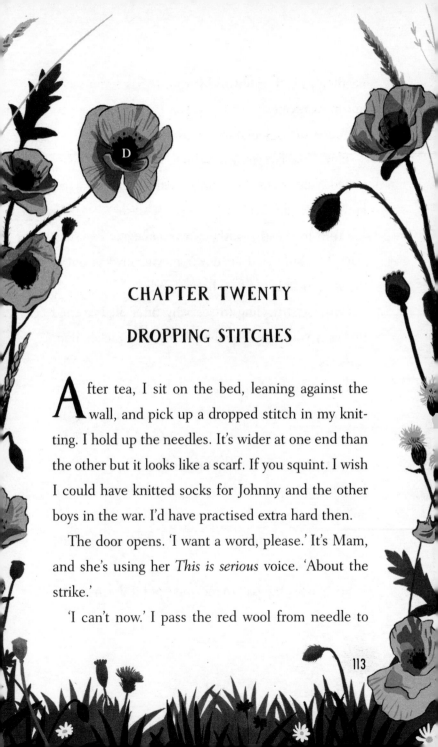

CHAPTER TWENTY

DROPPING STITCHES

After tea, I sit on the bed, leaning against the wall, and pick up a dropped stitch in my knitting. I hold up the needles. It's wider at one end than the other but it looks like a scarf. If you squint. I wish I could have knitted socks for Johnny and the other boys in the war. I'd have practised extra hard then.

The door opens. 'I want a word, please.' It's Mam, and she's using her *This is serious* voice. 'About the strike.'

'I can't now.' I pass the red wool from needle to

needle. 'I need to finish this row. It has to be much longer by my next knitting lesson.'

'You're still going to school on Monday then.'

'Of course I'm going to school. I'm twelve.'

'Don't be cheeky,' she says. 'And look at me when I'm speaking to you.'

I turn my head slightly, so I'm looking at her sideways. She huffs and sits down, moving my legs out of the way, making me face her properly.

'I'm just struggling to see why, after all I've tried to teach you, you're willing to cross a picket line,' she says.

'*Cross a picket line?* Mam, it'll be Nerys and Owen on the pavement on their own – and he'll only be there because Nerys will nag him to death if he doesn't! They'll look a right pair of fools.'

She picks up the wool ball and squeezes it. 'If you'd only let me explain how important these things are.'

'I don't want that getting tangled,' I say, holding out my hand.

She passes the ball to me and I put it down on the other side of the bed.

'You're always trying to explain. Trying to make me be just like you – and don't say you don't, because you do. Well, you can give up now.' I knit another stitch. 'You don't need to *enlist me to the cause*. You've got Nerys.'

Mam's mouth is open, like she's going to speak, but she closes it again. *Why isn't she saying she doesn't want Nerys?*

She sighs. 'If she understands, then why can't you?'

I stare at her. 'Because it's easy for Nerys – she can call a strike, make a fuss, in the end it won't matter if it fails because *she's* not going to lose her home. She knows that, Mam, deep down.'

'Oh, Natty …' She reaches for me, but I twist away.

'In fact, Nerys knows *everything*. Because she's the family genius, isn't she?'

A small voice comes from the landing, 'It's almost bedtime. Mam says there's Horlicks if you want some.' Nerys goes away again.

Mam glowers at me. 'Now you've upset your cousin.' She gets up. 'Happy now?'

Yeah, Mam. Happy as can be.

Two scruffy rows later, I start to calm down. Mam talks about teaching me, explaining things, as if I don't understand. But she never asks what's important to *me*, so then she thinks I don't care about anything.

But I helped Johnny remember Comforts, and I'm going to help him get his memory back. I might not be organising a protest, or listing demands, but I can make a difference.

I know I can.

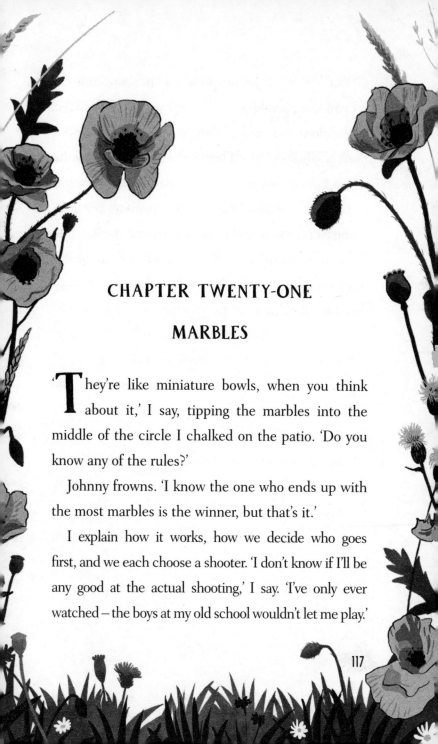

CHAPTER TWENTY-ONE

MARBLES

'They're like miniature bowls, when you think about it,' I say, tipping the marbles into the middle of the circle I chalked on the patio. 'Do you know any of the rules?'

Johnny frowns. 'I know the one who ends up with the most marbles is the winner, but that's it.'

I explain how it works, how we decide who goes first, and we each choose a shooter. 'I don't know if I'll be any good at the actual shooting,' I say. 'I've only ever watched – the boys at my old school wouldn't let me play.'

'You'll be good,' Johnny says, and he's so certain of it I can't help smiling.

We don't talk much, but we laugh a lot, and I wonder whether, if he'd been my age at my school, he would have let me play. He asks about the strike, and I tell him that Mam's been in her element all morning, giving Nerys ideas for the best way to organise it, while I had to do Nerys's jobs. But that's all I say, because I don't want to even think about it while we sit here flick-flick-flicking away, the morning sun warm on our faces. He's like a different person to the boy I first saw at the bus stop. His hands aren't even shaking.

Please let this be a way to help him know who he is.

'Ow!' I misfire my shot and scrape my knuckles on the flagstone. Tiny blobs of blood appear.

'Careful!' he says, and I'm about to say that I'm all right and there's no need to fuss when he adds, 'Don't get blood on the marbles!'

We laugh again. This must be what it's like to have a big brother.

Johnny wins the first match and I reset the game, humming a song I heard Aunty Mary singing yesterday. In half a minute, Johnny's humming along, head down, polishing his shooter marble on his trousers.

I stop. 'Do you know this song?'

He shrugs.

'You joined in.'

He sits back and looks into the distance. 'I did, didn't I? Fancy that!'

'Yeah.' I grin. 'Fancy that!'

By the time Lavinia and Charles come back from their stroll, it's a draw at two games each. Charles says that's the best way to end. We say goodbye and I promise to come back very soon.

As I walk away, Johnny starts humming again.

May Morgan's on the high street, coming out of the corner shop with a bulging paper bag. She takes out a handful of sweets and shoves them all in at once. I duck down the lane behind Hannah's bakery to avoid her. I'm just about to see if it'll lead me back to the high street when a scuffling sound makes me stop. The bin at the back of the bakery wobbles, and I freeze, expecting to see the biggest rat I've ever laid eyes on.

But no rats appear. Instead, a hand reaches up and dips into the bin. I step back and peep around the corner, thinking I'll find Albert Sullivan or his friend up to some mischief. But it's not them. It's Owen, and he's filling his pockets with old bits of bread – the things that didn't rise or were burnt. *What's he doing?*

He takes a bite out of one, and then I understand. He's taking the bread they can't sell so his family have something to eat.

I run away before he can see me, along the high street and up the hill to Fferm Fach, feeling wretched and uncomfortable and ashamed.

But most of all I'm angry. That feeling I had in the classroom, when Owen was punished and May was let off, flares up again. If I can help Johnny, I can help Owen and the others. It's not the same, but it's still unfair and, even though it doesn't feel like my fight, I can't stay out of it. Not after this.

I'm joining the strike.

CHAPTER TWENTY-TWO

ROUNDED UP

Nerys and Huw are in the yard. He's holding Sid Davey's puppy, it wriggles and tries to lick his face.

'The daft thing still doesn't know where he lives,' Huw says. 'A fine sheepdog he'll make with no sense of direction.'

'He probably wants to be in your workshop again,' I say.

Nerys stops playing with the dog's tail. 'He was in the workshop? When?'

'Yesterday,' I say. 'All cosy in some old sheets, like it was a nest.'

'Why didn't you call me to see him?' she asks.

'Because you were with Owen,' I say, ignoring the irritation in her voice. 'Do you know his name now?'

'Dad said Davey hasn't decided,' Nerys says sharply.

'No wonder he's here again.' Huw says. 'Can't train a dog if you can't call it, can you? He's twp, Davey is. There's sheep in his field with more brains than he's got.'

Nerys takes the puppy. 'He's so handsome.' She lets him lick her. 'I'd call him Douglas.'

'Well, there's a surprise,' Huw says, laughing.

'Why?' I ask.

'Douglas Fairbanks, isn't it? The film star. Nerys wants to marry him.'

She looks suddenly serious. 'I do.' She rubs her cheek on the puppy's head. 'Oh, Huw, talking of love – Mam said you had another letter today. Have you got a sweetheart?'

A sweetheart? Perhaps that's who wrote the letters I saw on his desk; the handwriting was quite feminine.

'Don't be silly,' he says.

'Is she pretty?' Nerys asks, batting her eyelashes and smiling in a mock-sweet way. 'Is she—'

'Just stop!' Huw snatches the puppy from Nerys. It yelps and tries to break free of his hold. 'See what you've done now? You've upset the pup.'

He marches over to the gate, the puppy squirming and yipping. Huw manages to open it, thrusts the little dog on to the track, then kicks the gate shut and storms off. It bounces off the latch and swings back-wards and forwards. Me and Nerys watch it till it slows to a stop.

'I'll get it,' I say. When I turn back, she's all stiff, like she's in shock. 'You didn't upset the puppy.'

Her voice wobbles. 'I upset Huw though, didn't I? I don't know how to speak to him any more.'

There's a scuffling noise from the other side of the gate and a black snout tries to push it open.

'I don't think he's going to go home on his own,' I say.

'You take him,' Nerys says, and I can tell she's upset and embarrassed about Huw.

'I don't know the way,' I say gently. 'You'll have to show me. This one obviously has no idea. Look at him!'

Little paws scratch at the ground, as if he's trying to tunnel to us. Nerys almost smiles, then sniffs and nods. For once, I feel sorry for her. I know it isn't Huw's fault, but it's not hers either. Johnny and Charles have been through terrible things – and are still suffering – but they're always kind. I wish Huw would stop taking it out on his sister.

Nerys scoops up the puppy and brings him into the yard. 'It's quicker this way,' she says.

We go past the house to the arched gate, and up the sloping orchard. The puppy's tail wags like mad under Nerys's arm.

I can't work out where we're going, because there doesn't seem to be anywhere *to* go. Nerys heads to the right of the back hedge and ducks down. 'Over here,' she mutters.

'This is my *secret* way up the Gweld.' She passes the pup to me, pulls back some branches, puts her free arm through and waves it around. 'See?'

The hedge is quite deep but the gap is big enough.

When we're on the other side, I put the puppy down and he runs around our feet, sniffing the grass. Nerys heads for a copse of trees. 'Douglas' races ahead of us, as if he now knows his way home. 'Davey's property is on the other side,' she says. 'Keep an eye out though, he's got a shotgun.'

'He's got a *what*?'

'A shotgun,' she says, all matter-of-fact. 'To protect his sheep. Oh, don't look so worried, he's never fired it. He calls it his Insurance Policy.'

Running through the field is fun, and even Nerys can't stay sad with the puppy tearing around. Every now and again he stops, turns fast and lies flat to the ground. 'Look, he's rounding us up!' I call.

Nerys shouts, *'Baaaaa!'* Then we jog slowly, pretending to be sheep, the little dog running around us, then flattening himself on the grass over and over, till we're both laughing ourselves silly.

'What are you two daft girls doing with my pup?' A short man wearing a battered hat, scruffy old waist-coat and baggy trousers walks up the field towards us.

It's like he saw a picture of a farmer in a book and copied it. Or maybe a scarecrow. If a scarecrow had a shotgun hanging from one arm.

'We're training him!' Nerys shouts back.

'By pretending to be sheep?' Sid Davey's out of breath by the time he reaches us. 'You're soft in the head, you two are.'

Nerys looks at me and says, *'Baaaaa!'* again, and we giggle. Sid shakes his head, then whistles for the puppy, who's more interested in rolling in some cow parsley.

'Come on, boy,' Sid says. 'I haven't got all day.'

'What's his name?' I ask, eyeing the gun. I don't like being so close to it, even if it isn't ready to fire.

'Dunno.' Sid shrugs. 'Takes no flaming notice of me, no matter what I call him.'

Nerys bends over and pats her knees. 'Douglas. Here, boy!' The puppy sits up, head cocked, then races towards her.

'Douglas?' Sid asks.

The puppy stops, cocks his head again, and runs to his master.

'Well, I'll be blowed,' Sid says. 'Douglas it is then.' He goes off whistling, with the puppy dancing round his feet. He stops to shout over his shoulder. 'Now clear off, you little trespassers!'

Me and Nerys laugh again and walk back to the house.

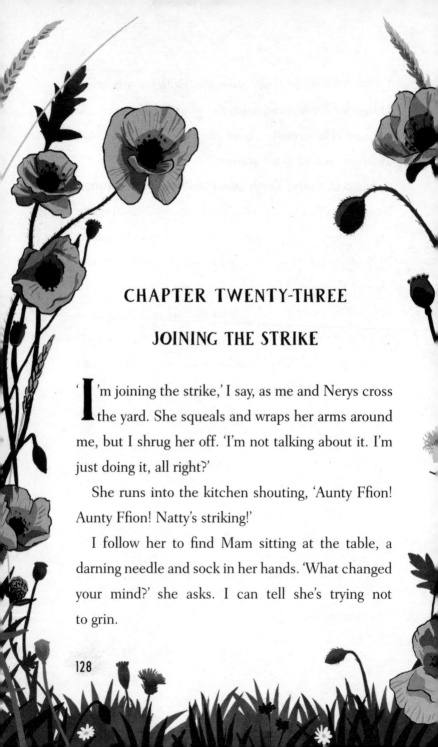

CHAPTER TWENTY-THREE

JOINING THE STRIKE

'I'm joining the strike,' I say, as me and Nerys cross the yard. She squeals and wraps her arms around me, but I shrug her off. 'I'm not talking about it. I'm just doing it, all right?'

She runs into the kitchen shouting, 'Aunty Ffion! Aunty Ffion! Natty's striking!'

I follow her to find Mam sitting at the table, a darning needle and sock in her hands. 'What changed your mind?' she asks. I can tell she's trying not to grin.

'Not you,' I say. Her smile disappears completely. 'I thought about it, that's all.'

Good. That ought to keep her from saying she told me so, or she's proud of me.

Nerys is beside herself. 'You can help make a banner. It's going to be the best one. I've made a list of possible slogans – Aunty Ffion helped me …' Nerys beams at Mam, but she's concentrating on darning the sock and doesn't look up. 'It's a long list – there's so much to say – and I need to choose just the right thing.'

'I can help with that,' I say.

'Oh no, I don't need you for that,' she says. 'I meant I need your help to paint it.'

'Charming. Perhaps we should make our own banners?'

Her bottom lip comes out like she's five. 'But it will take two to hold and carry mine. It's going to be big!'

Mam gets up. 'Nerys, perhaps Natty wants to make her own protest sign.' She looks at me. 'We can think of some slogans together if you like?'

'It's all right,' I say. 'I'll help Nerys. There'll be plenty of other signs.'

'Hooray!' Nerys says. 'It's going to be the best school strike ever!'

Mam sits back down to her mending.

I'm cutting some bread for dinner when Huw comes through the back door, just as Nerys walks out of the scullery, a tower of sheets and blankets in her arms. She's so small, only her eyes show over the top. Uncle Dewi stands behind her, wiping grease off his hands with a cloth.

She goes to rush past Huw, her whole body stiff again, but he reaches out and touches her arm. He tilts his head to show he wants her to come close to him and whispers, 'Sorry.'

It's like she melts. Her shoulders go down and her face softens. She kisses his cheek and practically skips out of the kitchen.

'Your sister's not been herself,' Uncle Dewi says to Huw. 'Any idea what's bothering her?'

Huw picks some paint off his shirt. 'Have you fixed the tap?'

His father nods.

'Mam'll be glad. She's been complaining about that drip for days.'

Uncle Dewi wipes his hands, watching his son. 'What happened, boy?'

'It's fine, Dad,' Huw says, walking into the living room. 'I said sorry.'

Uncle Dewi watches him go, then turns to me. 'Have you spoken to your mother, Natty?'

'Yeah, she knows about me joining the strike,' I say, putting the breadboard in the middle of the table. Leek and potato soup today. Lovely.

'I bet that cheered her up.'

'Why? What's wrong now?'

He looks at me funny, and I wish I hadn't said 'now'.

'I had to tell her last night that there's no job at the factory after all.'

'Oh, she never said.'

Probably because I've hardly looked at her since she started on about the strike.

'Don't worry, love,' he goes on. 'Something else might come up in a few weeks. It just means you'll have to stay here with us a bit longer, but you're always welcome. It's no bother at all.'

He smiles his nice, kind smile and gives me a cwtch. 'Might be an idea to be extra kind to your mam though. She was very disappointed.'

I nod, and he goes into the living room too. Now I feel bad for being mean to Mam when she was already upset. But how was I to know?

My hand hovers over the spoons in the drawer as I realise something. I don't mind at all that we're not going back to Libanwy. Fferm Fach is … well … it's nice, and we never have to worry about anything. I *want* to be here. Because of Johnny, because of Huw, and perhaps even because of the strike too.

I pick out six spoons. Things are changing and, until now, I never knew that could be a good thing.

CHAPTER TWENTY-FOUR

WHO'S WITH US?

Owen and Nerys have gone to tell 'a carefully selected few' at Sunday school and ask them to spread the word. But only the children they trust. Aunty Mary and Uncle Dewi walked with Nerys to chapel. Me and Mam stayed behind and peeled the veg for dinner. We never go to church or chapel. I think Aunty Mary was surprised, but she didn't say anything. Even though Huw's in his workshop and didn't go either. I went to see if Johnny, Charles and Lavinia were at the pavilion but it was locked up and empty. I suppose they're at church or chapel too.

I'm sitting on the field, running my fingers through the grass, when Nerys and Owen come up the slope towards me.

I jump up. 'Are many coming?'

'Yes,' Nerys says. 'Owen's rugby mates – Albert and Griff. I'm not happy about them, but we need numbers, and the other boys do what they say. And Maude Campisi and Ivy Beynon – they have plenty of friends.'

'Ivy Beynon?' I ask, remembering how pleased Nerys was when Ivy got her times table muddled.

'Ivy's all right. We have a *friendly rivalry*.'

'She's really clever too,' Owen says. 'Competition for the Brecon County School.'

Nerys twirls her hair, reminding me of how Johnny touches his pocket when he's fretful. 'Yes, well … she hates Mad Dog. So does Maude. That's what matters.'

Suddenly she runs in circles, flapping her arms and making a strange sort of whining sound.

'What are you *doing*?' I ask, staring at her.

'Probably saw a wasp,' Owen says. 'She's petrified of them.'

Nerys stops dead. 'Oh. It was just a bit of fluff on my cardigan.'

Owen laughs. 'Anyway, the most important thing is not to have any tell-tales until we know how many are on our side. So definitely not May Morgan.'

Children start appearing in ones, twos, small groups. In ten minutes, there must be about thirty. I keep to the back, out of the way. Nerys and Owen stand at the top of the slope. She claps her hands.

'Flipping heck,' says a girl next to me. 'If she's going to act like a teacher I don't care what she has to say, I'm off.'

The freckled, curly-haired boy she's talking to grabs her sleeve. 'Give her a chance.'

The girl huffs, but stays.

Owen shouts, 'Quiet!' and everyone stops talking. Nerys asks how many children have been beaten by Mad Dog Manford. Almost everyone's hand goes up, even the littlest children. I can't believe how many he's hit. He must spend all day with a cane in his hand.

'And why were you beaten?' she asks.

'Cos he's a git!' shouts another boy. Laughter spreads around the field.

'That's true,' Nerys says patiently, 'but what were your punishments for?'

'I dropped the inkpot,' says another girl. 'Got a swipe across my palm for that, and I had to scrub the whole floor, not just where the ink spilt. He did that on purpose because he knew my hand was killing.'

'I got into a fight with Griff,' Albert says. The boy next to him must be Griff, because he shoves him and they laugh.

Ivy puts up her hand. 'I smudged my slate! He gave me the paddle.'

'See?' Griff says. 'Even the clever ones like Ivy Beynon get it! It's not just us dunces.'

He shoves Albert back and they laugh again.

A voice calls from the top of the slide. 'What are you doing?'

Oh no. It's May Morgan. Just what we need!

Nerys folds her arms, lips pressed shut.

May screws up her face like the sun's in her eyes,

even though the sky is all clouds. '*I said*, what are you doing?'

'Mind your business, Morgan,' Griff yells.

May scowls. 'Well, whatever it is, it looks stupid to me anyway.'

Owen and Nerys share a worried look.

'I'll get rid of her.' Albert picks up a stone.

'Don't!' Nerys squeaks.

'I'm just messing,' he says. He spins his arm around as if he's bowling a cricket ball, but lets the stone drop to the ground. May looks around her as if she doesn't know where it went.

'I'm telling on you, Albert Sullivan!' she screeches.

'Duw duw, that'll make a change.' Albert rolls his eyes and laughs with Griff.

May whizzes down the slide and runs off, hat flapping like a giant cabbage leaf.

Owen watches her till she's out of sight, then takes a big breath. 'Who's ever been hit because they had no food in their stomach?'

The crowd shuffles, murmurs. There are a few shrugs.

'I mean because you couldn't think properly because you were so hungry.' His voice wobbles. He scans the faces looking up at him, aching not to be the only one.

More shuffles, more murmurs, some nods this time.

'Well, that was me on Friday.'

'Yeah!' Albert shouts. 'Seven of the best and the dunce's cap! Mad Dog was a right swine that day.'

Owen nods, his voice getting stronger. 'And I swear I could tell you all my tables right now – backwards if you like – but that's because of the Sunday school biscuits. And I know it's not just me.'

The girl who had to scrub the floor tries to speak, but has to do a little cough before the words can come out loud enough. 'When I dropped the inkpot, I … oh … it doesn't matter.'

'Go on, Maude,' Nerys says kindly.

The small girl holding Maude's hand pipes up. 'She was a bit woozy in the head. It's like that sometimes when you've had no supper and no breakfast.'

Others share the times Mad Dog clouted them for

forgetting the capital of France, or – in the small girl's case – having her buttons done up wrong.

'But what's this about?' Ivy asks. 'You haven't called us all here just to talk about bad things. What's going on?'

Nerys stands very straight and says, 'Children over in Libanwy get fed at school. For free. And we're going to make sure we get the same.'

'How?' shouts the girl next to me.

Nerys finds me in the crowd. I nod to her and mouth, *Go on*, and she declares, 'By going on strike!'

'You're mad,' Ivy says. 'Children can't go on strike.'

'They can.' Owen raises his voice over the rumbling chatter. 'It's been done before – and they've won!'

The crowd mutters and mumbles.

Now Owen claps his hands and they all go quiet. 'A strike,' he shouts, looking around at all the children and grinning. 'For proper dinners. Hot ones, with meat and gravy and puddings! Who's with us?'

The children cheer, some pump their fists in the air and others whoop. The curly-haired boy whoops the loudest. I don't think the little ones even know what a strike is, but they join in anyway. So do I, because this feels great. Like with Johnny, this feels like *doing something*.

Nerys and Owen start to share their 'battle plan'.

'Let's decide on what we're going to chant,' Owen says. 'This protest needs some noise.'

The children whoop and cheer again. I don't think noise will be a problem.

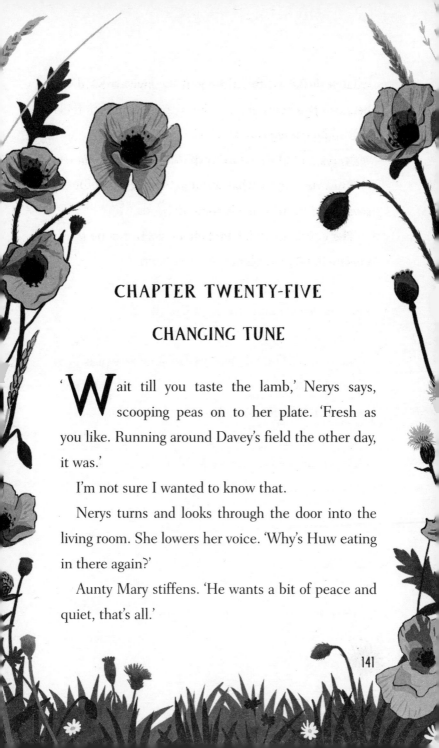

CHAPTER TWENTY-FIVE

CHANGING TUNE

'Wait till you taste the lamb,' Nerys says, scooping peas on to her plate. 'Fresh as you like. Running around Davey's field the other day, it was.'

I'm not sure I wanted to know that.

Nerys turns and looks through the door into the living room. She lowers her voice. 'Why's Huw eating in there again?'

Aunty Mary stiffens. 'He wants a bit of peace and quiet, that's all.'

141

'How did the meeting go?' Uncle Dewi asks. 'Did you get a good crowd?'

'Yes,' Nerys says. 'Thanks to Owen. He was great, wasn't he, Natty?' I nod, my mouth full of roast potato. 'Some of them are too scared to join in tomorrow because their mams and dads won't like it, but they promised not to tell on us. Everyone who wants to strike is making a sign or banner.'

'Wonderful,' Mam says, beaming at Nerys. 'And you're sure you can trust the non-strikers?'

'We're sure.'

Nerys and Mam talk like experts – using words I've heard Mam use so often at our own dinner table, but never really understood because I took no notice. Nerys has taken notice though. And Mam is delighted.

'I'm proud of you,' she says. 'All of you.'

I shrug, and ask Uncle Dewi to pass the mint sauce.

Aunty Mary is putting the plates in the sink when Huw appears in the doorway.

'There's no point, you know,' he says.

'Not now, eh, boy?' Uncle Dewi says. 'The girls are trying to do a good thing.'

He looks at his father like he's stupid. 'I'll tell you something, shall I?'

'Huw, I said *not now.*'

But it's too late.

'You're all deluded if you think anyone can fight the establishment. Schoolteachers, the council, the army top brass, they're all the same. They don't care about us. No one wants to feed Owen and the like, they're too busy making sure them and their own are all right. Ffion … you'd do well not to encourage my sister to think otherwise. She needs to learn what the world's really like.'

Nerys stares at the tablecloth, twirling her hair very fast.

'Leave it now, eh?' Aunty Mary pleads. 'Let's have some peace on a Sunday.'

Huw laughs grimly, turning to me. 'And *you've* changed your tune.'

Why is this suddenly my fault?

'Yes,' I say. 'I have. I'm allowed, aren't I?'

'Natty,' Mam says. '*Please*. We're guests in this house.'

'He started it.'

Huw eyes me in an odd way, like he's shocked and amused all at once. Everyone else just looks uncomfortable.

Aunty Mary's smile is so false, it's like it's painted on. 'I've got apple tart for afters.'

'I'm not hungry,' Huw says, walking into the living room and coming back a second later with his tray. He's hardly eaten a thing. 'See? Not hungry. I'm going to my workshop.'

Nerys turns over and the bedspread slips off me. I try to pull it back but she's got it wrapped around her like a caterpillar in a cocoon. I huff, and get out of bed to fetch another blanket. There's a tiny gap in the curtains where she didn't shut them properly so I go to do that too.

It's cold by the window, and a breeze comes through the frame on to my hand. Something moves down by the pigsty. I glance at Nerys but she's dead to the world. I pull the curtains together, so I'm peeping through the tiniest slit, very aware of my pounding heart.

Slowly my eyes adjust. There's definitely someone down there. Then they turn and, in the moonlight, I see who it is.

Huw.

He goes into his workshop and closes the door. I feel bad I snapped back at him. The first lines of that poem from my test booklet float into my head:

There are strange Hells within the minds War made.

I wish there was a way I could help him like I'm helping Johnny. But what Huw's lost, he can never get back. Perhaps I can tidy his paintbrushes again and we can talk about Rhys. He said no one else knows, which means I'm the only one he *can* talk to. It's probably not enough, but it's something.

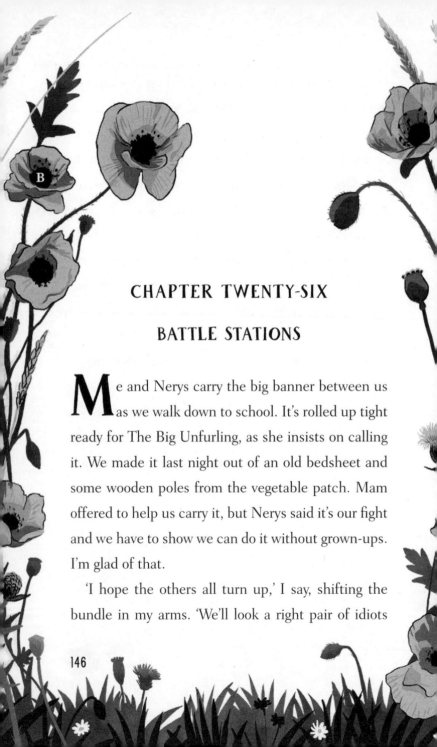

CHAPTER TWENTY-SIX

BATTLE STATIONS

Me and Nerys carry the big banner between us as we walk down to school. It's rolled up tight ready for The Big Unfurling, as she insists on calling it. We made it last night out of an old bedsheet and some wooden poles from the vegetable patch. Mam offered to help us carry it, but Nerys said it's our fight and we have to show we can do it without grown-ups. I'm glad of that.

'I hope the others all turn up,' I say, shifting the bundle in my arms. 'We'll look a right pair of idiots walking up and down the street holding this on our own.'

'We won't be on our own,' Nerys says. 'We've got Owen. And the others all like Owen.'

She's right, they *do* like Owen. He's what Mam would call a natural born leader. And it doesn't seem to worry Nerys at all that they aren't so keen on her. Her and Owen work like a peculiar little team.

We stand on the pavement in front of the railings. A few people say good morning as they pass.

'Oh heck, here's Prosser the Post,' Nerys says. 'He's so annoying.'

The postman stops – well, he's more like a post*boy* really. Definitely not much older than us. 'Good morning, young ladies.'

We both say hello.

'Just off to your house now, I am.' He points to his postbag. 'Got another letter for your Huw.'

'I can take it to him.' She holds out her hand. 'Save you going.'

'Oh no! I can't do that. That's tampering with the King's Mail, that is. An offence punishable by law.'

'I'm not going to open it! *That* would be tampering. You can give it to me, I'm his sister.'

Prosser eyes the hill. 'Well, it is a bit of a climb, and it's the only post I have to deliver up there today …'

Nerys's hand is still out. She wiggles her fingers. He digs in his postbag and takes out a letter. Dainty handwriting again.

'Thank you,' Nerys says, putting it in her satchel.

He nods towards the rolled-up banner. 'What's that?'

'Just you wait.' Nerys grins. 'Big plans. You'll never have seen the like.'

'Really? Well, I haven't got time to stay around here to see whatever tomfoolery you're up to, Nerys Williams.' He puffs out his chest. 'I'm in charge of the King's Post, I am.'

And off he goes. Nerys calls after him, 'Don't worry, I won't tell His Majesty you gave me the letter!'

He shouts something back about treason, but we're laughing too much to hear.

Voices drift up the street. Lots of them. Sounds like children. Then they appear, led by Owen like he's a general or something. Most of them are carrying signs or placards, and I can see a few more rolled-up banners. I glance sideways at Nerys. If any of them are bigger than ours, she'll be tamping.

More children arrive, from other directions. All buzzing like excited bees. We join together at the school gates and Owen organises us into groups. He stands back to check everyone's signs and banners are clear. 'Nerys, Natty – come and see this.'

The three of us stand together and survey the scene. A large crowd of children, big and small and in-between hold their banners and signs:

IF I LIVED IN LIBANWY
I'D GET FED AT SCHOOL

FREE SCHOOL MEALS NOW

VICTORY TO THE SCHOOLCHILDREN

WE SHALL FIGHT UNTIL WE WIN

DOWN WITH MAD DOG

That's Albert and Griff's – which Nerys says they'll have to change.

OFFICIAL PICKET

I think we can do this.

'I can't see Ivy or Maude,' Nerys says, looking around.

'They'll be here,' I say.

Some other children, a few I recognise from the meeting, stand away from us, ready to go into the playground. One of them, the boy with freckles and curly hair, gives us the thumbs-up. I wonder why he's not striking; he was really eager yesterday.

Further up the road, May Morgan leans against the wall, her arms folded. Watching.

Nerys says if children want to cross the picket line, we must let them. Peacefully. We can't give Mad Dog or the council any reason to break up this strike.

'Won't be long now,' she says. 'Mad Dog's going to get the shock of his life.'

Albert and Griff snigger.

'It's not meant to be amusing,' Nerys says.

'All right!' Albert pulls a face. 'Don't get your gigantic banner in a twist!'

'Don't be like that, boys,' Owen says. 'It's solidarity we need now. Not in-fighting.'

'Remember, everyone!' Griff shouts. 'Whatever we do, we mustn't be *amusing*!'

Nerys looks like she's about to lamp him one, until Mad Dog crosses the yard and opens the gate.

'Ready, Natty?' she says. I nod and we unfurl our banner.

EMPTY STOMACHS = EMPTY MINDS

Mad Dog stops dead for a second, then walks towards us, his face twisted with fury.

Owen begins the chant: 'What do we want?'

We reply, 'Free school dinners.'

'When do we want them?'

'NOW!'

'What is the meaning of this?' Mad Dog rages. Some of the smaller children cower, but Nerys stands up straight, her face defiant. Miss Phillips appears, looking panicked, but before she has a chance to speak, Mad Dog tells her to take the non-striking children inside, but to allow May to stay.

He looks at our banner. 'Tell me, Miss Morgan, is your father at home?'

May smirks. 'Yes, sir.'

'Then I shall pay him a visit. This is a matter for the council.'

'It is,' Owen says. 'They're the ones who need to give us our dinners.'

Mad Dog's fingers twitch and, for one second, I think he might hit Owen, but instead he turns and storms off up the pavement. May Morgan follows the others into school.

Owen lifts his placard into the air. 'What do we want?'

'Free school dinners.'

'When do we want them?'

'NOW!'

May watches us from the doorway, scowling from under her daft hat.

Nerys groans, and I turn. It's Ivy Beynon, with Maude and her little sister. And they're holding a banner that's bigger than ours, neater, and with the slogan:

FULL TUMS = CORRECT SUMS

Owen stares. 'Nerys! Ivy's banner is almost the same as yours.'

'No it isn't!' Nerys snaps.

'It is,' Albert says. 'Got the equals sign and everything.'

She huffs. 'Ours is cleverer.'

'Theirs is funnier.'

Griff puts his hands to his cheeks and pretends to look shocked. 'Oh heck, I think someone needs to tell Ivy and Maude we're not meant to be *amusing*!'

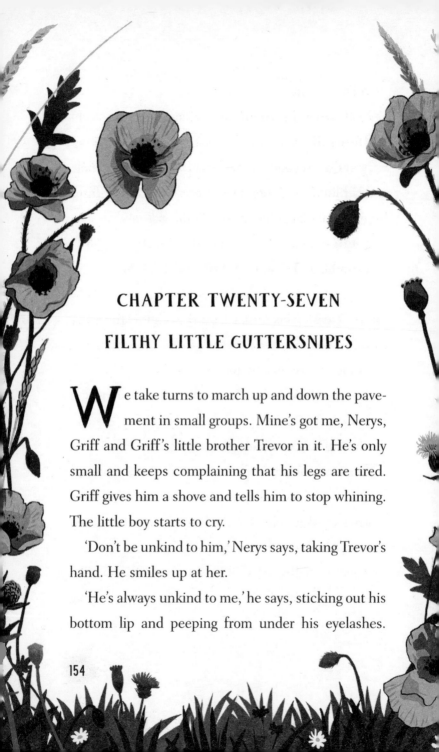

CHAPTER TWENTY-SEVEN

FILTHY LITTLE GUTTERSNIPES

We take turns to march up and down the pavement in small groups. Mine's got me, Nerys, Griff and Griff's little brother Trevor in it. He's only small and keeps complaining that his legs are tired. Griff gives him a shove and tells him to stop whining. The little boy starts to cry.

'Don't be unkind to him,' Nerys says, taking Trevor's hand. He smiles up at her.

'He's always unkind to me,' he says, sticking out his bottom lip and peeping from under his eyelashes.

'And I'm only five, you know.'

Griff shakes his head. 'Stop milking it.'

I feel really sorry for Trevor till he swings his leg back and aims a kick at his brother's shin. 'Take that, you filthy cur!' he shrieks, then runs off to hide behind Albert, who's laughing his head off.

'See? Gives as good as he gets, our Trevor,' Griff says, rubbing his leg.

By the church clock, it's almost quarter to ten when Mad Dog comes back up the road. He's with a short, round man who's wearing a suit and tie. He looks more curious than angry.

Owen and Nerys step forwards to meet them.

'Now now, what's all this then?' the man says, looking up at our banner. 'Who's in charge here?'

'*In charge?*' Mad Dog's face is a revolting shade of purple.' How can *they* be in charge of *anything*?'

'I'm in charge,' Nerys and Owen say together. They glance at each other, annoyed.

'Then I shall confer with you both,' Councillor Morgan says calmly. 'I see from your notices that this is somehow about food.'

'Yes,' Nerys says. 'We want free school dinners, like they get in Libanwy. Here is a list of our demands.' She takes an envelope from her apron pocket.

'*Demands?*' I think Mad Dog's head might actually explode.

Councillor Morgan sighs, and takes it from her. 'Mr Manford, we shan't get anywhere if we don't at least *listen*.'

Mad Dog glowers at us. 'What's the world coming to, when we listen to children? They need to be back in their classrooms. That's all there is to it!'

'Why don't you and I go into school, now, Headmaster?' Councillor Morgan says, waving the envelope and dipping his head to Nerys.

Mad Dog turns away, muttering under his breath. It sounds like *Filthy little guttersnipes*.

Half an hour later Morgan and Mad Dog haven't come back out. The children are still happily chanting and waving their signs and, as Owen says, *spirits are high*. Ivy and Maude are teaching Maude's sister the words to a protest song, and Trevor has charmed all the girls and kicked most of the boys.

Nerys waves across the road, and I turn to see Mam and Aunty Mary coming out of the corner shop.

Don't come over, don't come over.

Too late.

'How is it going, love?' Mam says.

'Good!' I say quickly. 'You don't need to stay.'

'I know,' she says, like she's trying to keep her patience.

'It's going wonderfully, Aunty Ffion,' Nerys gushes, practically pushing me out of the way. 'Councillor Morgan's here, and just *look* at everyone!'

Her and Mam watch the protestors with the same daft, dreamy-eyed expression. Aunty Mary just watches.

'Nerys! Natty!' Owen calls over the chanting. 'They're coming out!'

Mam's got that look in her eye. The same one she had at Litton's factory steps. 'Perhaps we ought to stay,' she says. 'See what this councillor has to say for himself.'

No, no, no! She'll ruin everything!

But Nerys looks more horrified than me. 'Oh no, Aunty Ffion, you and Mam can't stay – you'll undermine our cause. The whole point is that it's *our* fight. By the children, for the children. I'm sorry, but you need to leave.'

Mam's face goes red, but she nods. 'Yes, yes of course.'

Aunty Mary eyes me for a second and smiles, then kisses me and Nerys on the cheek and walks off up the road, with Mam looking back like every step is an effort.

The strikers all go quiet. Mad Dog and Councillor Morgan are at the gate. Me, Nerys and Owen push to the front.

'I've read this carefully,' Councillor Morgan says, holding the envelope out to Nerys. 'But I'm afraid the council cannot meet your demands. There is simply no budget for free school dinners.'

Nerys folds her arms, leaving the envelope in the councillor's stubby fingers, halfway between them.

'Please, sir,' Owen says, his voice level and calm. 'In Natty's last school, in Libanwy, they were fed.'

'We were – and the puddings were really nice!'

Why the heck did I go and say that?

Councillor Morgan's eyes flit to me. 'I'm sure they were delicious, but it's a matter of priorities.'

'Priorities?' The word bursts from Nerys. 'What's more important than this?'

Mad Dog leans over the councillor's shoulder. 'Miss Williams tends to believe her views ought always to be a priority.'

Councillor Morgan takes a deep breath. 'Children, it is my belief that your education is suffering far more from this strike than from lack of food. So I leave the situation in your headmaster's capable hands. But I suggest you have a *long, hard think.*' He looks around the crowd. '*All* of you.'

Some children, like Ivy and Maude, are looking more determined than ever; some shuffle and stare at the pavement; but no one moves towards the gates. With a nod to Mad Dog, Councillor Morgan walks away.

Nerys grabs a placard off Albert. The one that says WE SHALL FIGHT UNTIL WE WIN.

'Oi!' he says, rubbing his hands together. 'It's rude to snatch, mun!'

She pushes her way back through the strikers and starts to march along the pavement. She's got some guts, I'll give her that. Me and Owen look at each other, pick up our banner and join her. Soon, all the strikers are marching and chanting again.

And, when I dare to look, Mad Dog has gone.

CHAPTER TWENTY-EIGHT

MARCHING

Mad Dog keeps the other children inside at dinner-time, probably so they can't come and talk to us through the railings. It's not long after the bell goes when Owen nudges me and points at a woman crossing the road towards us. It's Hannah, and she's holding a wicker basket.

'This will be good!' Owen says.

He's right – Hannah's basket is full of gingerbread. 'Fresh out of the oven –' she beams – 'for all you little rebels.' She nods towards Nerys, who's marching her group back along the pavement. 'Well, look at this. And her only a little dwt an' all.'

I swear I can see Owen's chest swell with pride. 'That's our Nerys.'

Hannah laughs, and her whole face seems to shine with the joy of it. The children crowd round. 'Don't push,' she says. 'There's plenty for all.'

Me and Nerys organise everyone into a line and tap the hands that try to sneak in before their turn.

'Get off!' Albert scowls. 'I get enough whacks off Mad Dog.'

I'm last to take some. 'Thank you.'

'Right!' Hannah says loudly. 'I'd better get back to the bakery. You can take care of this, can't you?' She gives me the basket. 'Share the rest out, then bring it back after. Then you might get something else in it tomorrow.' She winks. 'Good luck!'

We carry on – marching and munching.

Suddenly Albert yells so loud that Trevor drops his gingerbread, but he doesn't seem to mind – he just picks it up and takes another bite.

162

Albert points across the road. 'Soldiers!'

Outside the Post Office, Johnny is standing behind Charles's wheelchair. Lavinia's queuing inside; I can see her cap.

Griff joins Albert. 'Let's see how many Germans they killed!'

They're about to step off the pavement when I grab them by their collars. 'Don't you *dare*!' I pull them back so hard they stumble.

'What the flaming heck are you doing?' Albert rages, rubbing his throat. 'You nearly throttled me!'

'And me,' Griff says, coughing.

'Leave them alone,' I say. It comes out like a snarl. I expect them to argue, to ignore me, even to laugh, but they look at each other, and Albert gives a little nod to Griff.

'All right,' he says. They shuffle away.

Owen appears next to me, grinning. 'You're scarier than Mad Dog, you are!'

'I must be,' I say, watching the boys huddling with their gang, clearly talking about me. 'I'll be back now in a minute.'

I cross the road. Charles and Johnny smile when they see it's me.

'I bet your headmaster doesn't like that,' Johnny says, waving a hand at the protest.

'Not one bit,' I say.

'What changed your mind? You were dead set against it on Friday.'

I shrug, slightly embarrassed at the fuss I made, only to end up striking anyway.

'Well, I admire your gumption, Natty,' Charles says. 'All of you. This is a most honourable endeavour. Just what those stuffy old men in suits need.'

Johnny's gone quiet, spellbound by the marching and the chants.

Two women pass us. They look across the road, tut and shake their heads, muttering about *disgraceful behaviour* and *unruly children*.

'Marching,' Johnny says. 'I remember marching.'

'Yes,' I say, grabbing his sleeve. 'You marched.'

Johnny only stares.

The Post Office door opens. Lavinia comes out and breaks the spell.

'Oh hello, Natty,' she says, putting some letters in the postbox. 'Are you striking after all?'

'Yeah,' I mutter.

'Good for you! Will we see you at the pavilion later?'

'Yes, after school,' I say. 'I've had an idea.'

'Another way to help our young scrap to remember?' Charles asks. I nod. 'Well, aren't you a marvel? Helping Johnny, shaking up the establishment!'

I shrug again, sure my face must be pink. No one's ever called me a marvel before.

We say goodbye and I cross the road.

Griff comes over. 'How many did they kill then?'

I glare at him. 'Oh, *shut up!*'

At the end of the school day, the children who went to lessons file past. The freckle-faced boy waves to us but doesn't stop.

'Who is he?' I ask.

'Peter Hopkins – the butcher's son,' Owen says. 'I think he'd join the strike, but his dad's not willing.'

'SCABS!'

Where's that coming from?

'DIRTY, FILTHY SCABS!'

It's Trevor.

'Be quiet!' Nerys yells. 'You don't even know what you're saying. Griff – take him home!'

May Morgan sneaks up to us. '*My father* says you're all going to be in so much trouble for this.' She looks overjoyed at the thought. 'He says you'll lose interest and give up before the week's out.'

'Oh, May,' Nerys says wearily. 'We aren't all like your family, you know – too lazy to fight for anything.'

May splutters. 'You … you … horrible little … I'm telling on you!' She storms off.

'Owen's coming home with us to do our grammar exercises.' Nerys pulls her satchel up on her shoulder. 'It's important to keep on top of our studies, even if we aren't all getting a scholarship.'

'Oh, Nerys, are you getting a scholarship?' Owen grins. 'I never knew!'

She nudges him in the ribs. 'Very funny. *You –*' she shoves the rolled-up banner at him – 'can help us carry this.'

'I'm not coming,' I say.

Nerys looks surprised. 'Why not?'

'I … I'm going for a walk first. It's been a big day and I want to get some fresh air – make room in my head for all the grammar.'

'You've been outside all day!' She narrows her eyes. 'You're quite strange at times, Natty Lydiate.'

But thankfully she leaves it at that; I don't want her sticking her nose in. Helping Johnny is something I can do all on my own.

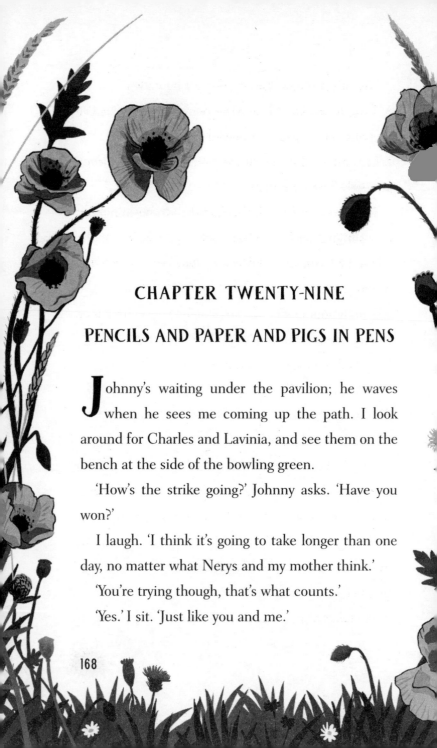

CHAPTER TWENTY-NINE

PENCILS AND PAPER AND PIGS IN PENS

Johnny's waiting under the pavilion; he waves when he sees me coming up the path. I look around for Charles and Lavinia, and see them on the bench at the side of the bowling green.

'How's the strike going?' Johnny asks. 'Have you won?'

I laugh. 'I think it's going to take longer than one day, no matter what Nerys and my mother think.'

'You're trying though, that's what counts.'

'Yes.' I sit. 'Just like you and me.'

168

'We are,' he says. 'So what's your new idea?'

I dig in my satchel for the pencils and paper I've brought. 'Have you ever played Pigs in a Pen?'

He raises his eyebrows. 'Natty, I can't even remember my own name, so how would I know?'

For a second I think I've said the wrong thing, but he's smiling, so I carry on. 'Some people call it the Game of Dots, or just Dots ... Anyway, this is what we do.'

I draw lots of dots in straight lines on the paper. Johnny leans over and watches me patiently. When I've filled the page, I hand him a pencil.

'Now, this is how to play. We take turns to join dots in horizontal or vertical lines – no diagonals.'

'No diagonals.'

I nod. 'The object of the game is to connect four lines to make a box. Then you put your initial in that box so you know you've won it. You've also won the right to go next. And it gets harder, but more fun, the more lines there are.' I look across at him. 'You can go first because you're new.'

He takes a pencil and draws a line.

Like with the game of marbles, we don't talk, we just play, sitting in the sunshine on the pavilion patio. Soon there are fifteen Js and twelve Ns on the paper.

'I wish I had my hat,' I say. 'It's getting really warm. Oh, I know!' I take a new piece of paper and start to fold it, back and forth, turning it over and over.

'Are you making a fan?' Johnny asks.

I nod, concentrating on the folds. It's a bit wonky, but it will do to keep me cool.

'I can do one better.' He takes another page and folds it in half. 'Watch this.'

He folds and smooths and makes the paper into squares and triangles until …

'A sailing boat!' he says, holding it up and grinning from ear to ear.

'That's brilliant!' I say. 'Is that something the nurses got you to do? To keep busy at Talbot House?'

'Nope.' Johnny leans back, turning the little boat over and over in his hands. 'I learned it when I was younger.' He scrunches his face up. 'Perhaps from my dad, or my uncle … or even my grandad.'

I stare at him.

He speaks slowly, as if straining to remember the exact person. 'I was taught by someone in my family.' He hands the boat to me. 'It doesn't really feel like remembering though … It's more of a feeling I know is true.'

'But it *is* true.' My voice comes out in a whisper, because of the lump in my throat. 'That's what matters.'

We stare at the paper boat in my hand.

'Play a game, draw a picture, then the memories might come back by themselves.' Johnny runs his fingers over his jacket pocket. 'That's what you said. And you were right.'

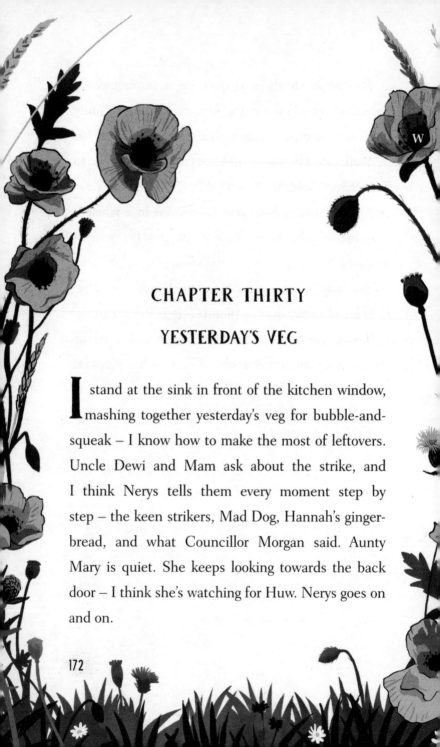

CHAPTER THIRTY

YESTERDAY'S VEG

I stand at the sink in front of the kitchen window, mashing together yesterday's veg for bubble-and-squeak – I know how to make the most of leftovers. Uncle Dewi and Mam ask about the strike, and I think Nerys tells them every moment step by step – the keen strikers, Mad Dog, Hannah's gingerbread, and what Councillor Morgan said. Aunty Mary is quiet. She keeps looking towards the back door – I think she's watching for Huw. Nerys goes on and on.

They probably think I'm smiling to myself about the strike, but I'm not. I'm smiling because Johnny knew how to make a paper boat.

'Well, all I'll say is this,' Uncle Dewi says to her. 'Keep fighting. Show them they can't wear you down. You shouldn't have any trouble with that, love.'

'You have to make more noise than anybody else,' Nerys says. *'You have to make yourself more obtrusive than anybody else.'*

'That's Emmeline Pankhurst!' Mam cries. I don't have to turn around to know she'll be beaming with delight.

'I finished the book.'

Oh no. Now they're going to go on about that. I smash the carrots and peas and potatoes together.

There's a noise outside, and the light from the workshop goes out. Uncle Dewi looks up. 'Sounds like the boy's on his way in.'

'Come on, young lady,' Aunty Mary says to Nerys. 'You can help me and your Aunty Ffion sort out which work clothes need mending.'

173

They go upstairs.

But Huw doesn't come straight in. He stops by the sty and leans on the fence, watching the pigs, his chin on his arms, and I wonder what he's thinking about. The war? Rhys? Perhaps nothing bad or sad at all. Perhaps just what's for tea …

Then –

There's an almighty crack, like the sky splitting open. It echoes round the valley like …

A gunshot?

Huw shouts, '*Get down!*' and drops to the ground. He's curled up against the fence, shaking, his hands over his head.

'What the hell was that?' Uncle Dewi says, running out of the door.

My heart thuds in my head. The saucepan slips from my fingers and clatters on the draining board.

Uncle Dewi rushes over to Huw. 'It's all right, boy, it's all right.' He holds him tight in his arms. Huw looks around, eyes impossibly wide, like he's terrified there'll be another shot.

I shouldn't be here. I shouldn't be watching this. But I can't move my feet.

Huw's yelling, 'Dad, make it stop! Make it stop, Dad!'

'It's all right, boy, I've got you. No one can hurt you now. You're home. You're safe.'

Huw buries his head in his father's chest and whimpers. It's the worst sound I've ever heard.

There's thudding on the stairs. Aunty Mary runs through the house and out of the back door. Nerys follows, but stops dead in the middle of the yard, twirling the ends of her hair really fast. She turns to look at me through the window. She's so scared.

I feel an arm slip around my shoulders.

Mam.

Aunty Mary comes back to her daughter, her face white. She doesn't say a word, just puts her arms around Nerys and pushes her back across the yard and into the house.

Mam's let go of me. She's at the door, her arms outstretched, and Nerys is passed to her like she's going to break.

By the look of her, I think she might have already broken.

'Let's go upstairs,' Mam says gently.

Me and Mam sit on the bed. We can't get Nerys to come away from the window. Or speak. Or even look at us.

'He'll be all right,' I say, and instantly feel stupid because … what do I know?

'He's got your mam and dad with him,' Mam says. 'That's good, isn't it?'

Nerys has her arms wrapped around herself, and I think if she squeezes any tighter she might pass out. She doesn't turn around, but does give a stiff little nod. I get up and look out of the window with her, my arm around her shoulders. Like Mam did with me. The workshop doors are wide open, and I can just make out the shelves inside. I think about me and Huw stroking the puppy, tidying up, talking about Rhys, and wonder if we'll get another chance. Nerys leans into me and I turn to see Mam smiling sadly.

Good girl, she mouths.

176

*

It's dark now but I leave the curtains open. I put my plate on the bedroom floor, the bubble-and-squeak hardly touched. I bet no one is eating in this house tonight. The door is shut, but sometimes sounds make it down the landing. Huw moaning or mumbling. Nerys crying in her parents' room.

The doctor came and gave Huw *something to help him sleep*. That's what he called it; I heard him from here. He's got one of those big voices that echoes around a place. If Huw can sleep through that, it must have been a very big dose of medicine.

Uncle Dewi's in with him. He told Aunty Mary he'll stay there tonight. I heard her take him a blanket. For if he falls asleep in the chair, she said.

I pull the covers up around me, and shiver, even though it's not cold. I never thought I'd think this, but I wish I didn't have the bed to myself. What's happening to Huw is shell shock. Aunty Mary said it's not the first time, but he hasn't had *an episode* – that's what she called it – for a long while. They'd all hoped that part was over. It was Sid Davey's gun that did it. Nerys said he's never fired it. But, for some reason, he fired it today. The doctor said it's taken Huw right back to the battlefields of Belgium, and Uncle Dewi said he's never really left, and I'm glad they couldn't see me because I cried. I thought about Huw and Rhys and Johnny and Charles, and I couldn't help it.

There's a click, and the door opens just a crack. Mam peers through. 'You're awake,' she says softly, coming in and closing the door again.

She pulls back the bedspread, slips in with me and holds me very tight, stroking my hair and saying nothing at all.

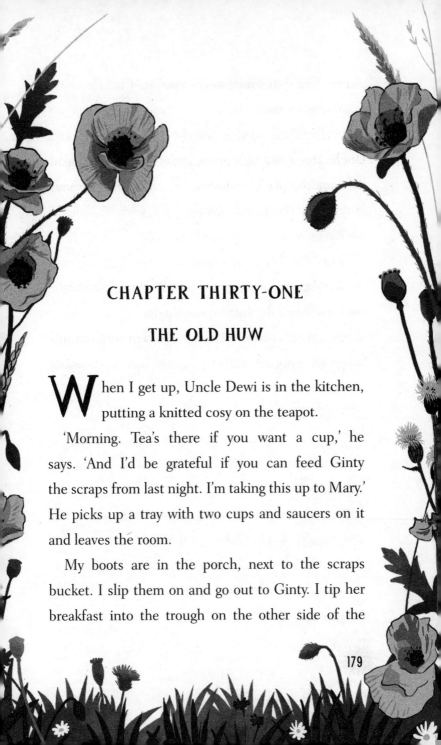

CHAPTER THIRTY-ONE

THE OLD HUW

When I get up, Uncle Dewi is in the kitchen, putting a knitted cosy on the teapot.

'Morning. Tea's there if you want a cup,' he says. 'And I'd be grateful if you can feed Ginty the scraps from last night. I'm taking this up to Mary.' He picks up a tray with two cups and saucers on it and leaves the room.

My boots are in the porch, next to the scraps bucket. I slip them on and go out to Ginty. I tip her breakfast into the trough on the other side of the fence. She trots over and happily tucks in.

'You're up early.'

I turn to see Nerys in the doorway. She's got a coat on, on top of her nightdress, and her hair's sticking up all over the place. 'I poured us some tea,' she says, holding up two metal mugs.

We sit on the chairs in the yard.

'I like tea in a mug,' I say.

'They're Dad and Huw's outside mugs.' She blows on hers. 'Mam'd go mad if she thought we were using them, says it's not ladylike, but Dad lets me have one when she's not around.'

She sips.

'I miss Huw,' she says.

I glance back to the house, suddenly worried he went to hospital in the night and no one's told me. 'Where is he?'

'In his room. I mean I miss the old Huw. The one who taught me to climb trees in there –' she points at the orchard – 'and who read me stories, and took me for all-day walks on the Gweld. When I was little, and he was playing with his friends, he always let me go

180

with them. He never left me out.' She scrunches up her face. 'Not like Sara.'

'I always wished I had a big brother,' I say. 'Not a sister though.'

She looks up at me. 'Girl cousins are all right though, aren't they? Like a friend, only better.'

I think of how Owen seems to be the only friend she has at school. The others either tease or tolerate her. Till now, I didn't think she minded.

'Yes, girl cousins are all right.'

She smiles, and it feels nice to have made that happen. She's not so bad. Not really.

'I've been thinking about these letters he's getting,' she says.

'The ones he keeps in the workshop?'

She nods. 'The handwriting is so delicate, I'm sure S. *Smith* is a girl. I wonder if she could help.'

'Perhaps she already does.' I think about what he told me about Rhys. 'Sometimes it's easier to talk to people you aren't as close to, because they ... I don't know ... they won't get upset or worried by some of the things you feel.'

Or expect you to be the same as you were before you went to war and lost your best friend.

She frowns and wrinkles her nose. 'That makes no sense.'

And, to Nerys, I suppose it doesn't. Everything is black and white to her. Right or wrong. Simple. Just like Mam. 'He's all right sometimes though, isn't he? I mean, he was really happy when you got all your spellings right.'

'That was great,' she says. 'That was like having my brother back.' She looks into her mug. 'The war took him away, Natty. And it gave him back, only not every part of him. And it took away some of the good parts, and gave him bad ones instead. He was never like this before the war. Not even once. You'd have really liked him then.'

'I really like him now,' I say.

She smiles, but shakes her head. 'He's not the same.'

I tell her about Johnny and Charles – I think I do it so she knows Huw isn't the only one. She listens really carefully and doesn't interrupt once. When I've finished, she asks, 'Are they the soldiers you went to talk to yesterday, outside the Post Office?'

'Yes.'

'Albert and Griff are such idiots about the war. They just don't understand that it wasn't an adventure.'

'I didn't realise you knew what happened yesterday.'

'I saw you grab Albert and Griff by the scruff, and Owen told me why.' She swigs her tea. 'The nurses bring the soldiers into the village to go to the shops and mix with people, which is nice when they meet people like you.'

I smile.

'But some treat them differently. They ask questions about the war, or they want to shake their hands and thank them, and Huw hates that. It's why he stays close to home.'

'I don't blame him,' I say. 'But Johnny can't stay close to home, can he? Not if he doesn't know where it is.'

'Do you think the war took all of Johnny away?' Nerys asks.

I think for a minute – about him, and the tag he keeps in his pocket, and the things he's starting to remember. 'No. No, I don't.'

'I wish I wasn't so useless.'

'You? Whatever happened to Dad-says-I-can-do-anything-I-want, cleverest-in-the-family, top-of-the-class Nerys Williams?'

'That's different. That's easy.' She looks across the yard at the workshop. 'It's only school.'

I nudge her. 'The school you're going to change forever – you and Owen – by getting us all free dinners. That's not useless.'

She smiles, keeping her eyes on the workshop. 'Not just me and Owen. You too.'

'Yeah.' I take her mug and stand up. 'Me too.'

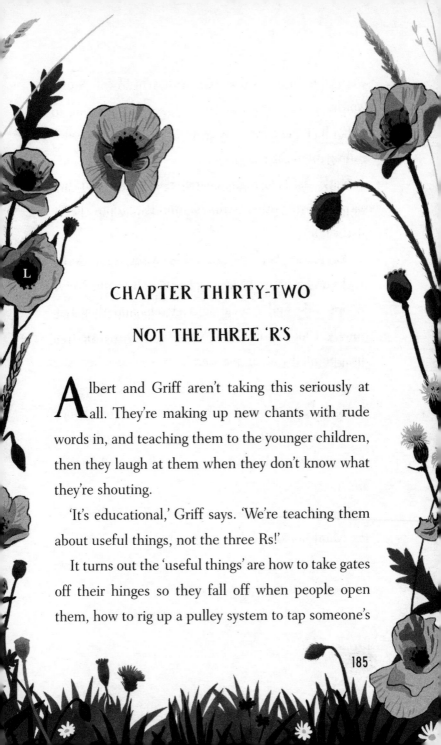

CHAPTER THIRTY-TWO

NOT THE THREE 'R'S

Albert and Griff aren't taking this seriously at all. They're making up new chants with rude words in, and teaching them to the younger children, then they laugh at them when they don't know what they're shouting.

'It's educational,' Griff says. 'We're teaching them about useful things, not the three Rs!'

It turns out the 'useful things' are how to take gates off their hinges so they fall off when people open them, how to rig up a pulley system to tap someone's window with a metal washer, and a lot of new swear words.

By half past nine, they have all the little ones calling them 'sir'.

Nerys isn't trying to stop them – which has surprised the other strikers, but they don't know about Huw.

We've been here about an hour when Aunty Mary ducks under Ivy and Maude's banner. She pulls Nerys to one side and into a tight cwtch, and they talk quietly. I look around for Mam, and, this time, I'm disappointed not to see her. It was nice when she looked after me last night.

Now Aunty Mary has Nerys's face in her hands and is smiling in that serious way grown-ups do when they want you to believe things are all right when they aren't.

A quiet voice comes from behind me. 'Hello, love.' It's Mam, looking a bit awkward. 'I know you don't want me here, but your Aunty Mary wanted to check on Nerys and, well, I wanted to check on you.'

I feel awful. My own mother is nervous to come

and see me. 'It's not that I don't want you here, it's just—'

'I know,' she says. 'You have your own reasons for doing this. You don't need me telling you what to do.'

Does she really mean that? Is she finally understanding?

'I got us some tinned peaches for tonight,' Mam says, holding up a shopping bag. 'Be lovely with a drop of evaporated milk.' She reaches into her coat pocket and pulls out a paper bag. 'And these – gobstoppers. One each for you girls and Owen. Although I think it might be a good idea to give them to those boys.'

Albert and Griff are climbing on to the school wall. The younger boys are cheering and egging them on.

Mam winks, kisses me on the forehead, and goes off up the street with Aunty Mary.

I turn to Nerys. 'How's Huw?'

'Resting,' she says, as if that's the end of it.

It turns out that Albert and Griff are having a competition to see who can lean back furthest, holding on to the railings. First one to let go is the loser. Owen goes to tell them to stop.

'They're so stupid,' Nerys says to me. 'Mad Dog's not going to forget everything that happens here. It's like they want to get beaten every day once we've won the strike.'

'What about us?' I ask. 'He won't let us forget either.'

'But we're following strike protocol!' she says, as if that makes everything all right. 'Peaceful protest. No criminal damage.'

Albert and Griff are taking no notice of Owen. 'We're not *in* school,' Albert shouts, his arms shaking with the effort of holding on. 'He can't tell us off now.'

'Want to bet?' Owen says.

Mad Dog's dashing across the yard. Albert and Griff jump off the wall and try to hide behind some other children.

'Sullivan! Watkin! What do you think you're playing at?' Mad Dog seethes, his purple face striped by the black railings. He looks like a cartoon prisoner, only there's nothing funny about this.

188

'Nothing, sir. Sorry, sir,' Albert says, not so cocky now.

'Damaging school property is *a criminal offence*,' Mad Dog says. 'If I see you – *any* of you—'

'No one damaged the wall,' Owen says. 'Or the railings.'

'I'd watch my tone if I were you, Elias.'

Nerys rushes over. 'Leave him alone, you big bully!'

The strikers gasp. Mad Dog's eyes widen. Albert splutters a laugh.

'*What* did you say?' Mad Dog asks. His voice isn't loud, but somehow everyone hears.

'Nothing,' Nerys lies, her cheeks burning red.

Mad Dog watches her for a few seconds, then walks away. I have a feeling that's the scariest thing he could have done.

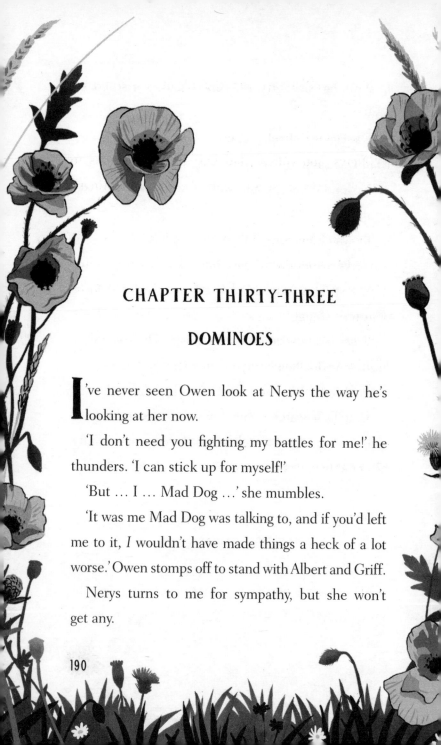

CHAPTER THIRTY-THREE

DOMINOES

I've never seen Owen look at Nerys the way he's looking at her now.

'I don't need you fighting my battles for me!' he thunders. 'I can stick up for myself!'

'But … I … Mad Dog …' she mumbles.

'It was me Mad Dog was talking to, and if you'd left me to it, *I* wouldn't have made things a heck of a lot worse.' Owen stomps off to stand with Albert and Griff.

Nerys turns to me for sympathy, but she won't get any.

'He's right,' I say. 'You've made it harder for all of us.'

'I haven't. I was just—'

'Nerys! You called Mad Dog a *bully*! Thanks to you, we'll have *no* school dinners and *more* beatings!'

'Thanks to *me*?'

'Yes!' I throw my hands in the air. 'All your bossing everyone around and showing off – it's like you've forgotten why we started this. You say it's about doing the right thing, but it looks to me like it's about you being the winner – top of the class at striking – even if it hurts the people you're meant to be helping!'

'That's not true!'

I don't believe it. She really can't see what she's done. 'Of course it's true!' And, even though I know she's upset about Huw, and I really ought to leave her be, I still say, 'I'd have thought *Little Miss Brecon County School* would know that!'

'You're *horrible*!' she splutters. 'I wish you'd never come here.'

'Then you'll be very happy to know I'm getting away from you.'

I leave her next to the railings, her face bright pink. There's only one place in Ynysfach I want to be.

I head for the park, glad to leave the strike – and the strikers – behind. What were we thinking? We're only going to make school worse. Huw was right: we're never going to beat the likes of Mad Dog and Councillor Morgan. We're just children.

Johnny's playing dominoes with Charles. He looks up as I get closer. 'What's the matter?'

I stare down at the patio, clenching and unclenching my fists. Seething.

'Want to talk about it?' he asks.

It's like turning on a tap – no, a waterfall! 'It's Nerys. She's driving me mad. Telling us all what to do, thinking she knows everything! And the trouble is, she has people like *her* father and *my* mother saying she's wonderful all the time! She's in for a huge shock when this strike fails, and Mad Dog is worse, and all the others hate her!'

Charles puffs out his cheeks. 'I'll … erm … I'll just see if Nursey needs a hand with the tea and cake.' He wheels himself off into the pavilion.

'Sit down,' Johnny says quietly. 'Tell me what happened.'

I explain about Albert and Griff and the railings, and Owen and Mad Dog, and Nerys's stupid, stupid outburst.

Johnny just listens, turning a domino in his hands.

'She doesn't see the cost of her actions. She thinks she's making things better, but it's other people who'll get hurt the most.' I take a massive breath and let it out. 'Nerys flipping Williams! She's just like my mother! They both – '

I stop.

Johnny has this odd look on his face, like he knows what I'm thinking – what I'm feeling – better than I do.

'Is it Nerys you're angry with, or your mam?'

'What? No!' I say. 'Nerys was wrong. And Owen's going to pay the price and … I know what that feels like, that's all.'

Which means I *am* angry at Mam. I flop on to the table, making the dominoes jump, and press my face

193

into my arms. He's right, and I should hate that, but in a way it's nice to have someone who understands me. I look up.

Johnny's straightening the dominoes.

'Stop being so wise!' I splutter, almost laughing and almost crying at the same time.

He shrugs. 'Can't help it.'

I do laugh now, then sit up and help with the dominoes.

Johnny puts his hand on my arm. 'Make up with Nerys.'

Lavinia and Charles come out of the pavilion. 'Oh,' she says, looking at the little upside-down watch she has pinned to her uniform. 'You're not normally here at this time.'

'She fancied a walk,' Charles says. 'Didn't you, Natty?' I nod, glad I haven't embarrassed myself in front of Lavinia as well. 'Now let's finish this game.'

Charles beats Johnny, then I beat Charles. I think he let me win. Usually that would make me cross, but today I don't mind at all.

194

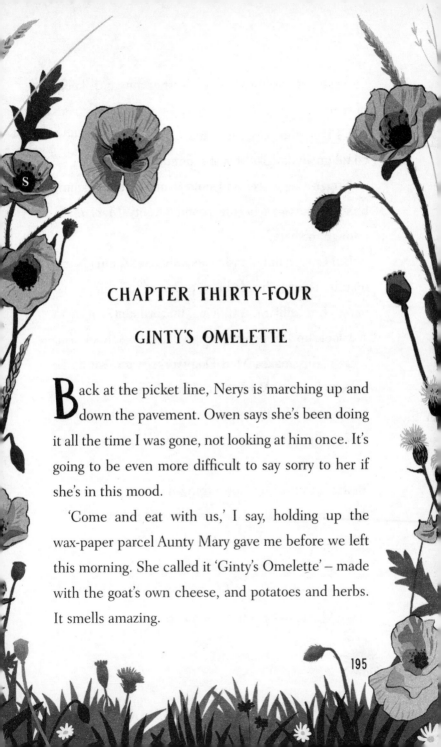

CHAPTER THIRTY-FOUR
GINTY'S OMELETTE

Back at the picket line, Nerys is marching up and down the pavement. Owen says she's been doing it all the time I was gone, not looking at him once. It's going to be even more difficult to say sorry to her if she's in this mood.

'Come and eat with us,' I say, holding up the wax-paper parcel Aunty Mary gave me before we left this morning. She called it 'Ginty's Omelette' – made with the goat's own cheese, and potatoes and herbs. It smells amazing.

Nerys sticks her chin in the air and keeps marching.

I sit on the pavement and Owen joins me. 'She could go all day like this,' he says.

I open the parcel and hold it out to him, hoping he's not going to be too proud. 'Aunty Mary made enough to share.'

But Owen smiles and takes a slice, watching Nerys march. 'Her pig-headedness is one of the things that makes her brilliant. Annoying, but brilliant.'

I look up through the railings to the school. 'But what if this makes Mad Dog worse when we do go back to lessons? What if he hits you more?'

'I expect he will, but that's not a reason to give up. Nerys taught me that.' He picks some parsley out of his omelette and squeezes it between his fingers. 'Being hit's not the worst thing he does anyway. My dad sometimes gives me a clip round the ear, but he never calls me names and sits me in the corner with a dunce's cap.' Owen eats the parsley. 'Nerys doesn't get it so bad because she's mostly in Miss Phillips's class. Going to be someone, she is.'

I smile.

'Mad Dog doesn't like Miss Phillips helping her though – he doesn't want children from factory families to better themselves. And, this year, he's tamping that the only scholarship entrants are girls.' He licks his fingers. 'Oh, here's Hannah with her basket again. Might be more gingerbread.'

It's pikelets.

Prosser the Post strides up the pavement behind Hannah and mutters, 'You really shouldn't encourage them, you know.'

Hannah turns. 'Haven't you got the Second Post to deliver?'

'Well, yes, but I'm only pointing out that these children ought to be—'

'Michael Prosser, it wasn't so long ago you were in short trousers snivelling in my shop because your mam wouldn't buy you a *third* cake, so you don't need to point anything out to me.'

Prosser flushes red, then scuttles off, clutching his postbag tightly.

Hannah watches him go. 'Meddling little toad.'

She heads back to the bakery.

The children all crowd round Owen and the basket.

Nerys is sitting on her own by the gates. I go over and offer her the omelette again. She takes it, but won't look at me.

'I'm sorry,' I say.

She sighs. 'Just leave me alone, Natty.'

I twty down. 'No. No, I won't. Because today was the worst day to quarrel with you. I really am sorry.'

She opens the wax parcel and stares at it for a minute. 'All right. But you have to be extra kind to me from now on.'

I sit next to her. 'From now on? How long is that?

'Possibly forever.' She giggles, her face scrunching up.

I nudge her. 'Don't push your luck.'

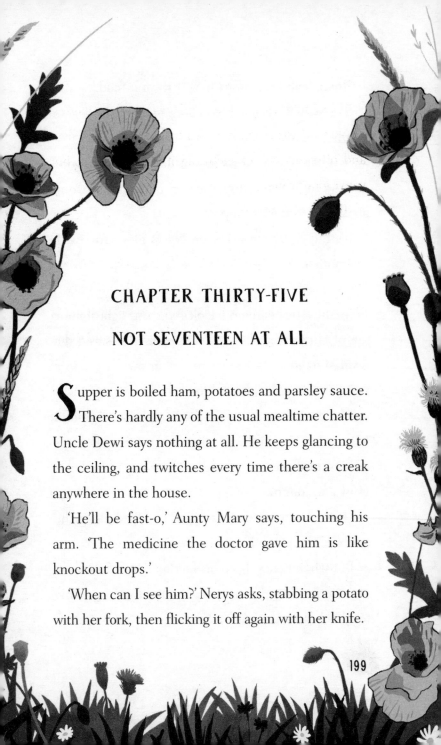

CHAPTER THIRTY-FIVE

NOT SEVENTEEN AT ALL

Supper is boiled ham, potatoes and parsley sauce. There's hardly any of the usual mealtime chatter. Uncle Dewi says nothing at all. He keeps glancing to the ceiling, and twitches every time there's a creak anywhere in the house.

'He'll be fast-o,' Aunty Mary says, touching his arm. 'The medicine the doctor gave him is like knockout drops.'

'When can I see him?' Nerys asks, stabbing a potato with her fork, then flicking it off again with her knife.

'Soon, love – and don't play with your food.'

She scowls. 'But I hate *doing nothing*! I want to help!'

'You can help your mam and dad by being a good girl and eating your supper so they don't have to worry about you too,' Mam says.

It's the first time I've seen Nerys look cross with my mother.

From the attic bedroom, I look at the soft light shining out of Huw's workshop. After supper, Nerys said she wanted to go and sit in there on her own. I suppose she wants to feel close to him.

The grown-ups are all in the living room. I think I left my knitting in there; I'll go and fetch it. Perhaps concentrating on something will help me, like it helps Huw and Johnny.

Huw's bedroom door is open, so I pad along the landing, extra quietly, in case he's snoozing.

But when I pass, I see his feet on a little footstool. He's in the chair. I'll just peep around the door frame to check he's all right. I haven't seen him since it happened, and I can't get his look of terror out of my mind. If I can see his face again – and he's calm – I might feel better.

He looks up straight away. So much for peeping.

'Hello.'

'Sorry,' I say. 'I was just … I'll go. Sorry!'

'It's all right.' He smiles. 'You can come in. I hope I didn't frighten you yesterday.'

'You didn't,' I say quickly, stepping just inside the door. 'It was you I was worried about. Are you feeling better now?'

'Yeah. But not because of those.' He points to the tablets on his bedside table. 'I've been telling Dad about Rhys.'

'Really? Oh that's brilliant! What did he say?'

'That he wishes I'd told him before.' There's something in his hand. He turns it in his palm and gazes at it. '*I* wish I'd told him before.'

'Well, he knows now.' I step closer to his chair. The thing in his hand is oval-shaped and on a metal chain. Oh, it looks like … 'Is that your identity tag?'

He blows out a breath, long and hard. 'No. Mine's

buried somewhere in the Passchendaele mud. With Rhys.'

'Then whose—'

'It's his.'

'I don't understand.'

'We swapped them, the first time we were called to the front line. Lots of boys did it, when they had a special mate. It was a sign of solidarity, brotherhood, I suppose. And we didn't swap them back because it felt like if we did, then it was bad luck. Can you believe it? Relying on luck in that place!'

'I can, because what else did you have?'

He rubs his thumb over Rhys's name. 'Each other.'

'May I see it?'

He hands the tag to me. It's a bit scratched, but the lettering is clear:

RHYS CILGERRAN JONES
METH
11·4·17
W·G·

I don't know what METH means, or those letters after the date, but it's set out just like Johnny's tag. Although the back is flatter, with one of those stamps that shows it's made of silver.

'I'm glad my tag's with him, even if I can't be.'

He reaches for his glass of water, but his hand is shaking so I get it for him. He smiles, but it's bitter. 'State of me, eh?' He takes a sip. 'Sometimes I wish it was me instead of him so I wouldn't have to miss him so damn much. Is that the most selfish thing you've ever heard?'

'No.'

But it might be the saddest.

I give him the tag back. 'Budge up,' I say, and sit on the arm of the chair. 'Tell me what you miss.'

Huw looks surprised, but he shuffles to one side to give me more room. 'What do I miss?' he says quietly, looking at the tag. 'Just knowing he's there. Having a laugh, arguing about rugby – different teams, see – talking about girls, making things. He always said my art was good. Said I could have been a war artist.'

'You could!'

Huw smiles. 'He used to get me to draw pictures on the letters to his girl.'

'Rhys had a girl?'

'Yeah.'

'Her heart must be broken.'

He rubs his thumb over the tag again. 'Mostly what you miss when someone is gone are the small things, the everyday ordinary things. And …' His eyes flick to me and away again. 'I miss how Rhys helped me not to be scared.'

I'm afraid to speak in case I cry. Huw's not crying and Rhys was *his* friend. I want to give him a cwtch but I don't know if I ought to, so I put my hand on his arm and he lets me leave it there.

'From the very first day, he seemed to know what I was thinking. I was standing by my bunk at Chelsea Barracks, wondering what the hell I'd done in signing up, and Rhys said, "For King and Country, eh?" and he had this look in his eye and I knew we'd be friends. The others used to call us the Taff Twins.'

204

'Did you look alike?'

He smiles. 'No, but we were cut from the same cloth, do you know what I mean?' I nod. 'And we were the youngest there, even though we'd never admit it, and always together. There was one day, out in Belgium, the weather was warm and we were lying in a field near some woods – all of our regiment – like it was a day trip to the seaside or something. Men sat in small groups around their rifles which were set up like little wigwams. I had to go into the woods for, well …'

'A wee?' I ask.

Huw bursts out laughing. 'I was trying to be polite but, yes. Anyway, when I came back I couldn't see my wigwam, couldn't see where Rhys was, and I panicked. It was odd – like the whole war was swirling around my head and I suddenly knew I'd never be the same again if I lost him. Then I heard a shout and a laugh, and there he was – waving me over, making fun of me because I'd been standing there like a stunned rabbit.' Huw's face darkens. 'Then it started, the tap-tap-tapping of hammers on wood.'

'What was it?' I whisper, a bit scared to know the answer.

'They were making coffins for those of us who'd need them.'

A cold tingle runs through my whole body and I squeeze his arm tight. How is anyone supposed to cope with that?

Huw holds the tag up on its chain. It swings in front of us like a hypnotist's watch. 'Sometimes I hear that tapping when I try to sleep. It used to happen every night. It's less now, but I don't think it'll ever stop.'

We watch the tag.

I take a big breath. 'When you were scared, what did Rhys used to say?'

'Different things.'

'The next time you're scared, if you think of what he would say, it might help.'

A few seconds pass, and I'm nervous I said the wrong thing, but when he looks at me, he's smiling. 'And they say Nerys is the clever one.'

I shrug and smile back. 'Don't say that to her.'

I want to ask him what the letters on the tag mean: METH and WG. But I look at him in that chair, with a blanket over his knees, not looking seventeen at all, and I think he's talked about it enough.

As soon as I get back to my bedroom I find a piece of paper and a pencil and write down what it said on Rhys's tag. Because there's someone else who might be able to answer my questions.

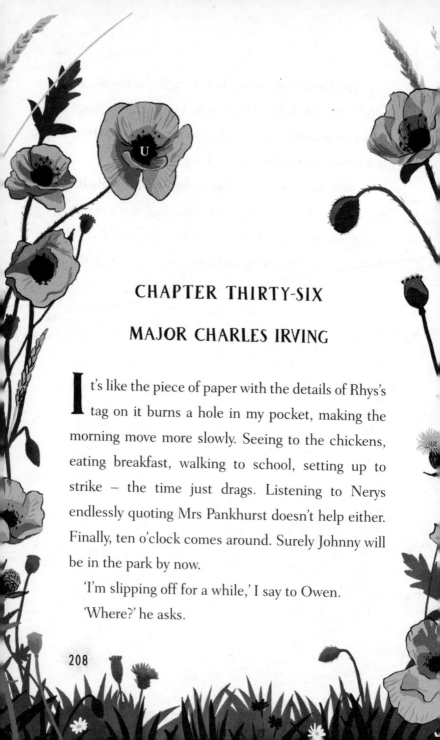

CHAPTER THIRTY-SIX

MAJOR CHARLES IRVING

I t's like the piece of paper with the details of Rhys's tag on it burns a hole in my pocket, making the morning move more slowly. Seeing to the chickens, eating breakfast, walking to school, setting up to strike – the time just drags. Listening to Nerys endlessly quoting Mrs Pankhurst doesn't help either. Finally, ten o'clock comes around. Surely Johnny will be in the park by now.

'I'm slipping off for a while,' I say to Owen.

'Where?' he asks.

'Can't say. Sorry. But it's important.'

'What's up with you two today?' he asks. 'She's being all secretive as well.' He points across the road to where Nerys is posting a letter.

'Aunty Mary was writing to Sara last night, it's probably that.'

'But she was—'

'Sorry! Got to go!' I run off, not stopping till I reach the path to the pavilion. Lavinia and Charles are on the patio, but I can't see Johnny.

I slow to a fast walk, trying to get at least some of my breath back before I reach them. Maybe Johnny's in the pavilion, or at the side of the bowling green.

Charles spots me and waves. 'Here's our girl!' he yells.

'Hello.' I look around. 'Where's Johnny?'

'He's not coming today,' Lavinia says.

'Oh.' It's like all the air goes out of me. 'Why not?'

'He's got … erm … a check-up.'

'All day?'

Lavinia and Charles share an odd look, like there's

something they don't want me to know. 'These things can be tiring, Natty,' he says. 'Even for a young scrap! Now, would you like a cup of tea?'

I look in the direction of school. 'I'd better get back to the strike – it was Johnny I needed to see. I wanted to ask him something.'

Charles holds his chest in a fake dramatic way. 'You wound me to the quick, dear girl.'

'I didn't mean … I'm sorry … I wanted to look at Johnny's identity tag again.'

'Take no notice, Natty, he's being a rotten tease,' Lavinia says.

'I'm a scoundrel!' Charles winks. 'But I know a thing or two about tags. Might I be able to help?'

'I've got this,' I say. I sit down and take the paper out of my pocket. 'It's copied from a real tag but I don't understand what all the letters mean.'

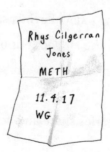

Charles takes it and reads. 'Who's Rhys Cilgerran Jones?'

'He's – he was – a friend of my cousin Huw. They were at Passchendaele together. I know Johnny has a similar kind of tag – it's the same shape and I think the writing is in the same place. If I can find out what these parts mean –' I point to the second and fourth lines – 'perhaps it will help us know what was on Johnny's.'

'METH stands for Methodist,' Lavinia says, from over Charles's shoulder. Most tags have the soldier's religion marked on them. In case, well …'

'So they could have the right burial service,' Charles says. 'You can say the words, Nursey. It's just a practicality. We weren't milkmen, we all knew we were doing a job we might not survive.'

I glance at Lavinia, who looks uneasy.

'What about the last line?' I ask. 'They look like initials but they don't match the name.'

'That's the regiment,' Charles says. 'The Welsh Guards.'

I take the piece of paper back. 'That same line on

Johnny's tag is short too, and the second letter might be a G. If WG is Welsh Guards, could he have been a Guard too?'

'A *Guardsman*?' Charles says. 'It's possible, but there's more than one regiment in the Guards Division. And many different kinds of tags too. What does this tag of your cousin's look like? Made of metal?'

'Silver, I think.'

He nods thoughtfully. 'And was it worn on a chain around the neck?'

'A bracelet.'

'Hmm … there were a lot of those. Known as "private purchase" discs,' he says. 'Unofficial tags. The boys had them made themselves. Didn't always trust the fibre ones they were issued. Too flimsy, especially if they got wet.'

'So Johnny's tag was specially made too?'

'Must have been.' Charles reaches into the front of his shirt and pulls out a chain with a round tag on the end. 'Here's mine.' He takes it off and passes it to me.

Charles points to each part. 'There's my rank and my name – Major Charles Irving. C OF E is Church of England, and that's my regiment. Fifth Bedfordshires.' He sits up very straight. 'And I was proud to serve with every last one of them.'

I turn the tag over in my hand. It's not far off looking new; more like Rhys's than Johnny's. This tag came out of the war better than Charles did.

'I've got an idea,' I say. 'But it might be a bit … silly.'

'I'm sure it's not,' Charles says.

'All right … so … if we can put the tags next to each other, maybe we can work out if they were in the same regiment and … and … perhaps Huw could help Johnny. I know there's only a small chance, but we might be able to find someone who knows him.'

'Then you must get to it right away!'

'But … oh I can't, not yet,' I say, 'The doctor says Huw's got shell shock. See? I told you it was silly.'

'It's not silly to want to help,' Charles says. 'Shell shock? We've had a fair few of those at Talbot House, haven't we, Lavinia? Terrible business. A broken body is one thing.' He waves a hand to his face and legs. 'Difficult as it is, the doctors know what to do with that. But a broken mind …'

I hold Charles's tag so tightly it hurts my hand. 'I want to help them both … but it feels impossible.'

Charles reaches out. I think it's to take the tag back, but instead he puts his hand over mine and squeezes. 'Shall I tell you what I felt was impossible?'

I nod.

'Escaping the trenches, winning the war, getting home alive. But here I am, Natty. Here I am.'

'Here you are,' I say. 'And I'm so glad.'

He beams.

'Thank you,' I say, getting up. 'You've both been very helpful, but I need to get back to the strike.'

'Will you speak to Huw?' Lavinia asks.

'When he's stronger, yes. Yes, I will.' I picture him sat in his chair. 'I don't know how long it will take, but it isn't as if I'm going back to Libanwy, so I can carry on helping Johnny till then, can't I?'

Lavinia and Charles share that odd look again.

'What?' I ask.

'Nothing,' Lavinia says, checking her watch. 'Goodness, is that the time? We'd better think about getting back to Talbot House for dinner.'

But Charles sees the look on my face and says. 'The girl's not stupid, Lavinia.'

'*What?*' I ask, more urgently now. 'Why are you looking at each other like that? Is something wrong with Johnny?'

'He's fine,' Charles says. 'A new specialist doctor wanted to see him.'

'But, if he's fine, then why does he need a new doctor? What's wrong with *your* doctors?' I know

215

I'm sounding rude, but I don't care. The panic is rising too hard and too fast. 'What are you not telling me?'

Lavinia sighs. 'It's good news, really.'

Her face is saying otherwise.

'Johnny's doing so well with all these sparks of memory, one of our doctors spoke to a specialist about his case. And the specialist wants to include Johnny in a medical trial at his clinic.' She glances at Charles, who's watching her carefully. 'In London.'

'London?' I sit down hard in the nearest chair. I know what this means, but I ask the question anyway. 'He's going away, isn't he?'

'More than likely,' Lavinia says quietly. 'But you do know it's for the best, don't you? This specialist is top in his field. He could help Johnny to—'

'But *I'm* helping him!'

These sparks of memory, they happen because of me.

'You are,' Charles says, leaning towards me, speaking softly. 'You really are, dear Natty, but you aren't a doctor.'

Saying it kindly like that doesn't stop it hurting. I want to shout, '*I know I'm not a flipping doctor! I'm only a girl! But I've still done more than they have!*'

Instead I just whisper, 'I know.'

Walking back to the strike, my heart actually hurts. I ought to be pleased. This might be Johnny's chance to discover who he is, to find his family. Which is all I want for him … isn't it? Then why do I feel so wretched?

Perhaps he won't go. Perhaps he'll choose to stay in Ynysfach.

And, I feel awful for thinking it, but I want him to. I don't know how to be here without him.

CHAPTER THIRTY-SEVEN

POLICE BUSINESS

Huw has his breakfast on a tray in the living room. He's fed up of being in his bedroom, and just having him downstairs makes the rest of us feel better. He even says he'll go in his workshop today.

Huw recovering makes me feel a bit better about Johnny too because, if I can ask Huw to help, maybe Johnny won't have to leave.

Me and Nerys carry our banner down the track and along the roads to school. We're almost there when we round the bend to find a crowd next to the high part of the school wall. At first I wonder why the strikers have gathered there. Now I notice most of the people are grown-ups, not children. We give each other a very nervous look and start to run, awkwardly, with the banner bouncing in our arms.

No one sees us coming because they're staring at the wall. Some of them are pointing. It feels like *all* of them are talking. Some words stand out from the noise and fuss.

'*Shocking* ...'

'*Disgraceful* ...'

'*Hooligans* ...'

'*Vandals* ...'

'What's going on?' Nerys asks the woman next to her.

The woman steps back like Nerys is poisonous, then shouts, 'Here she is! This is the one who started it all!'

Heads turn, people frown, some mutter and grumble. Adult arms sweep children out of the way, and now we see it. Written on the wall in big, white, painted letters:

MAD DOG MANFUD IS A GIT

I gasp – I can't help it. I glance at Nerys, but it's like she's frozen. Our banner falls to the ground. The sound is like an explosion in all the quiet. A black-shoed foot comes down on it and breaks the wooden poles with an echoing snap.

'Ah, Miss Williams, Miss Lydiate,' Mad Dog says. 'So good of you to join us.' Nerys still doesn't move. His eyes flick to the street behind us. 'We'll see what the officials have to say about this, shall we?'

I turn to see Councillor Morgan and a policeman rushing over, with May bumbling along behind her father.

'See, Daddy?' she says. 'I told you it was *awful*.'

'Stand aside,' the policeman says, his face serious. Everyone except Mad Dog obeys. The constable looks at him. 'I said stand aside, Mr Manford, if you don't mind.'

'But, Constable Davies, this is my school. I feel I must—'

'This is *everyone's* school, Mr Manford.' He sounds

like he's trying to keep his patience. 'And this is a police matter, so for the third time, stand aside, sir.'

I like Constable Davies already.

'Out of my way.' Mad Dog shoves past Peter Hopkins, who pulls a face behind the headmaster's back, which is brave with all these angry grown-ups around.

The policeman goes to the wall, touches the paint, then taps his fingertips to his thumb. 'Completely dry,' he says. 'I expect the culprit did it under cover of darkness.'

'So what happens now?' Councillor Morgan asks.

Constable Davies takes a notebook and pencil out of his pocket. He doesn't say anything for a few minutes while he writes. Nerys is trembling, so I link my arm through hers. 'I'll make a full and thorough investigation. Rest assured I'll get to the bottom of this.'

'It'll be all right,' I whisper to Nerys.

She takes a deep breath, staring at the words on the wall. 'How? How can it be all right now?'

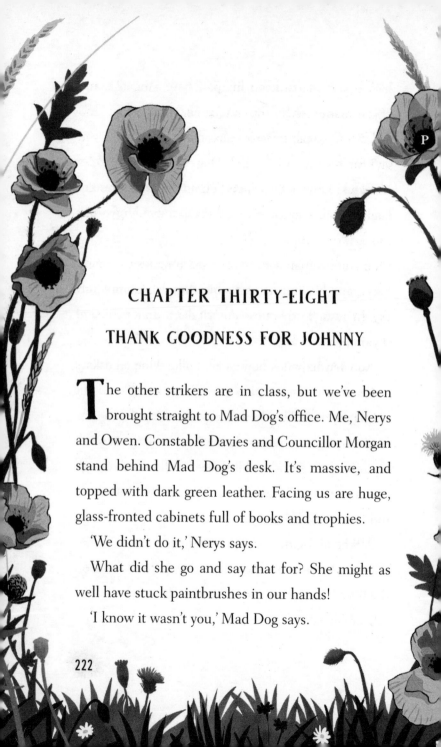

CHAPTER THIRTY-EIGHT

THANK GOODNESS FOR JOHNNY

The other strikers are in class, but we've been brought straight to Mad Dog's office. Me, Nerys and Owen. Constable Davies and Councillor Morgan stand behind Mad Dog's desk. It's massive, and topped with dark green leather. Facing us are huge, glass-fronted cabinets full of books and trophies.

'We didn't do it,' Nerys says.

What did she go and say that for? She might as well have stuck paintbrushes in our hands!

'I know it wasn't you,' Mad Dog says.

'Me and Natty were in my house all night and Owen was in his – you can ask our mams and dads.' She stops, frowns. 'Oh, erm … what did you say? Sir.'

'I *said* I know it wasn't you. Miss Williams, you are many things – opinionated, arrogant, insolent – but you are not stupid. You would have known that to daub such words on school property would result in the termination of the strike and your expulsion from Ysgol Ynysfach, therefore dashing any hope you have of gaining a scholarship to the Brecon County School.'

'And I wouldn't have made the spelling mistake,' Nerys says.

I fight to keep in a nervous laugh.

Mad Dog's voice is a growling whisper. 'Opinionated, arrogant, insolent.'

Constable Davies looks at Owen. 'The Sullivan and Watkin boys – you're a pal of theirs, I think?'

'Albert and Griff?' Owen shifts his feet. 'We play rugby together sometimes.'

'Did they say anything about this to you?' the policeman asks.

'No, nothing,' Owen says. 'I would have tried to stop them.'

'We all would,' I say.

'But you feel it is possible for the graffiti to be their handiwork?' Mad Dog asks.

Me, Nerys and Owen look at each other and I know we're all thinking the same thing.

'Answer me,' he says. 'Is it possible?'

Silence.

Mad Dog stands, his fists on the desk, he leans forward.

'Yes!' Nerys blurts out. 'It's possible, but there's no proof. You have no proof.'

'Not yet, not yet,' Mad Dog says with a horrible smile. 'That will be all.'

We're waiting outside the office, as we've been told, when someone comes out of the girls' toilets further down the corridor. It's May Morgan, looking over-joyed. 'You're in for it now,' she mutters as she passes.

'Oh, shut up, Cabbage Head!' I say.

Owen splutters with laughter, just as Miss Phillips arrives.

'Something funny, is there?'

Owen stares at the floor, his shoulders still shaking. 'No, miss.'

'This is for the best,' Miss Phillips says as she guides us down the corridor. 'The strike couldn't go on indefinitely and education is very important. Especially yours, Nerys.'

I want to ask Miss Phillips why she thinks me and Owen are less important, but I already know the answer – we're not scholarship material.

'Oh, I'm sorry, miss, but I'm not coming back to class,' Nerys says. 'You don't need to worry about my education though. I'm keeping up with my studies at home, but we can't stop now. The fight continues. We need to get back to the picket line.'

But, back outside, there's only the pavement, abandoned signs, and our banner, lying by the wall, dirty and battered.

'It's looking a bit sorry for itself, isn't it?' Owen says.

Nerys picks it up and tries to unfurl it, but the poles are broken and it just flops sadly. I know how it

225

feels. She grabs a placard instead. 'Come on, if we show willing, the others will come back.'

Me and Owen don't move.

'What?' she says. 'Look at this placard. Look what it says! WE SHALL FIGHT UNTIL WE WIN!'

'Nerys, there are three of us,' Owen says quietly. 'Everyone else is in class. Even Albert and Griff.'

'For now,' she says, like she's in control, but her voice is high and panicky. 'We'll show them. Come on. Look, you grab that one. VICTORY TO THE SCHOOLCHILDREN, that's a good one. Natty, which one will you have?'

I reach for a sign. Owen scuffs the ground and the sole of his shoe flaps.

'Owen?' She's almost frantic now. '*Come on!*'

He looks at her. 'There's no point. We tried, but it's over.'

'No ... Think of the free dinners. Think of defeating Mad Dog ...'

He speaks softly. 'Nerys, we've lost.'

'How can you say that?' she shrieks. 'This was all for you!'

Owen blinks like she stung him, which, in a way, she did. 'I don't need your charity,' he says. He walks off. It turns into a run at the street corner.

I put the sign down. Nerys looks at me, her eyes full of tears. 'I've done it now, haven't I?'

I screw up my face. 'I hate to say it but, yeah, I think you have.'

She sits on the pavement, surrounded by placards and signs and buries her head in her knees. 'Damn Albert and Griff and their stupid gang,' she mumbles. 'Stupid.' She throws a stone at the wall. 'Blinking.' Another stone. 'Idiots.'

I tidy all the signs into a neat pile, then hold out a hand to her. 'Let's go for a walk.'

'All right,' she says, in the smallest voice I've ever heard her use. I help her up and give her hand a little squeeze.

'We'll go to the park.'

'To see if your soldiers are there?'

'They're not my soldiers, but yeah. It might cheer you up. Charles can do magic tricks.'

'I like magic tricks,' she says, looking eager. 'Of course, I usually know how they're done.'

'*Of course you do,*' I say.

Lavinia and Nerys watch closely and gasp at Charles's magic. I was expecting simple card tricks but he's really good. Nerys bounces in her seat. 'Johnny's turn now. Do the one where he has to find his card, Charles! The one you did for Lavinia, when the card was in her handbag all the time! I want to watch it again. I'm sure I've almost worked it out.'

'You can't work it out,' Charles says. 'It's actual magic.'

Nerys frowns at him. 'They're called card *tricks* for a reason, you know.'

'It won't work,' Johnny says. 'I haven't got a handbag.'

'No, but you've got a pocket. Oh, you're both so funny,' Nerys says. 'Cheering me up, you are. Natty said you would. You said that, didn't you, Natty? Oh!'

Her whole body goes stiff.

'What is it?' Lavinia asks. 'What's the matter?'

Nerys's eyes flick to the back of her hand. And then I see it – not a bit of fluff this time. A brightly striped wasp crawling on her skin, its antennae feeling the way. Nerys breathes heavily through gritted teeth.

Johnny, Charles and Lavinia stare at her.

'She doesn't like wasps at all,' I say.

'*Nnnnnn.*' Nerys starts to tremble. 'Get it off, get it off, get it *off*!'

Charles raises a hand to swipe at it but Nerys shrieks and Lavinia grabs his arm. 'Just stay still and it won't sting you.'

Nerys stares across the park, her eyes wide. 'I can feel its legs.' She breathes in and out really fast.

Johnny leans forward and says to Nerys, 'See that patch of daffodils over there?' She nods quickly. 'Count how many there are. Out loud. Can you do that?'

She nods again, just once. She starts to count but before she's even got to two, Johnny blows the wasp away with one quick puff. Nerys's shoulders drop and she rubs her hand. 'Thank you,' she whispers.

'I didn't know you were *that* scared of wasps,' I say, marvelling at how Johnny calmed her down.

'Thank goodness for our young scrap, eh?' Charles says. 'Saved the damsel from a vicious beast!'

Yes. Thank goodness for Johnny.

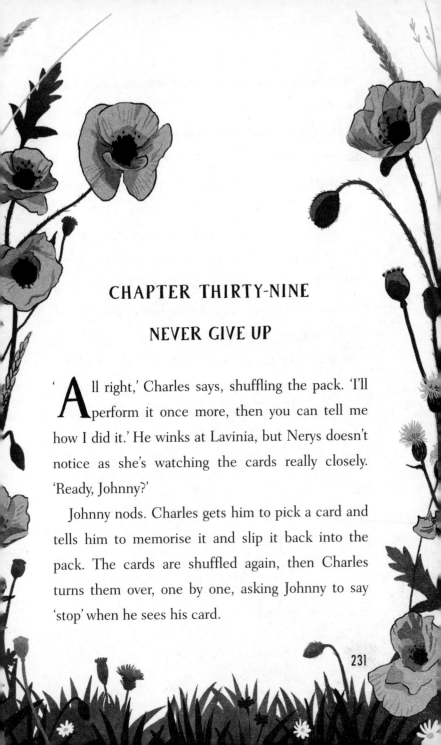

CHAPTER THIRTY-NINE

NEVER GIVE UP

'All right,' Charles says, shuffling the pack. 'I'll perform it once more, then you can tell me how I did it.' He winks at Lavinia, but Nerys doesn't notice as she's watching the cards really closely. 'Ready, Johnny?'

Johnny nods. Charles gets him to pick a card and tells him to memorise it and slip it back into the pack. The cards are shuffled again, then Charles turns them over, one by one, asking Johnny to say 'stop' when he sees his card.

But he gets to the end and Johnny still hasn't said 'stop'.

'Check your pocket! Check your pocket!' Nerys squeals.

Johnny looks at Charles. 'Go on,' the older man says. 'Left-hand breast pocket.'

That's the one where Johnny keeps his tag. He reaches in and pulls out first the tag, then the card.

We all clap and Charles takes a bow. Straightening back up, he nods at something in the distance. 'What the devil's going on there?'

It looks like Constable Davies is fighting with a bush at the side of the path. His arms are buried deep inside it, and he's grunting. He's trying to pull some-thing out of it. A different bush, further away, shakes. Leaves fly off and twigs snap as Griff bursts out and runs away.

'Best give in now, boy,' Davies says, huffing and panting, his helmet tipped to one side. 'Your pal's run off and left you – there's no escape now.'

He steps back, dragging an arm with him. Albert Sullivan stumbles from the bush, his clothes and hair

232

in a mess. In one quick movement, Constable Davies grabs hold of Albert's collar and lifts him so high he's hanging on his tiptoes, like a marionette. Then he marches him off down the path.

'Well, I never!' says Lavinia, her hand on her chest.

'I thought they'd gone into school,' I say.

'They're both for it now.' Nerys pulls a face. 'Griff can't hide from Constable Davies.'

'What's that all about?' Charles asks.

'They did some awful graffiti on the school wall,' Nerys says. 'About our headmaster. Said he's a – well … a very rude word. I mean, it's true, but you can't go around painting it on walls, can you?'

Charles laughs.

'And why did they do that?' Johnny asks.

'They're always up to something,' Nerys says. 'And they've broken the law before. Bull roaring the vicar's drainpipe. Had their backsides tanned for that by their dads, they did.'

'What's bull roaring?' I ask.

'Stuffing newspaper up and then lighting it,' Johnny says. 'Goes like heck. I used to do it.'

We all stare at him. He blinks. 'I just remembered.'

Lavinia speaks softly. 'Can you remember anything else?'

Johnny scrunches his eyes closed tight and rubs his forehead. 'No. Nothing. I just know that I did it.'

'We learn something more about you every time Natty's here,' Charles says. 'And it seems you were a very naughty boy!' He roars with laughter.

'I must have been.'

'But Albert and Griff have spoilt the strike,' Nerys says.

'Oh,' Charles says. 'That's not so funny.'

'No,' I say.

Nerys sighs. 'And we don't know what to do next.'

'I'll tell you what you *don't* do.' Charles leans forward in his chair. 'You don't give up. Never give up.'

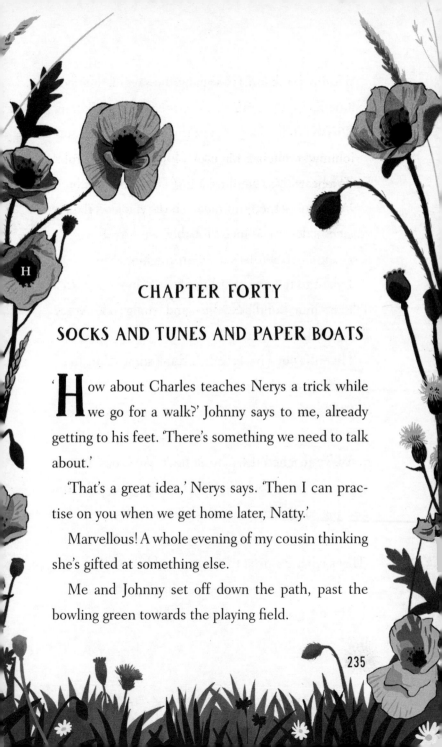

CHAPTER FORTY

SOCKS AND TUNES AND PAPER BOATS

'How about Charles teaches Nerys a trick while we go for a walk?' Johnny says to me, already getting to his feet. 'There's something we need to talk about.'

'That's a great idea,' Nerys says. 'Then I can practise on you when we get home later, Natty.'

Marvellous! A whole evening of my cousin thinking she's gifted at something else.

Me and Johnny set off down the path, past the bowling green towards the playing field.

'I know you know I'm leaving,' he says.

I nod.

'I wish I didn't have to, but this specialist, he's sure he can help. He's very keen … apparently.'

'When will you go?' I ask.

'As soon as they can organise the paperwork.' He glances sideways at me. 'Probably in a few days.'

A few days? So that's it. I've run out of time.

I want to tell him that I don't want him to go, that I'll miss him, but that's selfish and wrong so I just say, 'Will you be all right, in London?'

He puffs out a big breath. 'I think so. It's time to try something new.'

'Will you write to me?'

'Of course.'

We've reached the playing field. We cross it, then sit on the slope, looking down on some little children chasing each other with dandelions.

'If you pick one of those, you wet the bed,' I say. 'That's what we used to say at my old school.'

Johnny nods seriously. 'Scientific fact, that is.'

He tugs at some grass at his feet. 'Having you

as a friend has changed everything, you know. I've remembered so much since we met – and it's all thanks to you.'

All thanks to me.

Thanks to me, Johnny might recover.

Thanks to me, he's leaving.

I sigh. 'We've found some good memories, haven't we? Socks and tunes and paper boats.'

'Don't forget bull roaring drainpipes.'

We both burst out laughing.

'Natty,' he says. 'It's not just the memories you've helped me find. It's the feeling of having things to look forward to. So life's better, no matter what I remember. You did that too.'

'Really?'

'Really.' He looks across the field, and over the trees to the pavilion roof. 'Now let's get back to poor Charles before Nerys wheedles all his magic secrets out of him.'

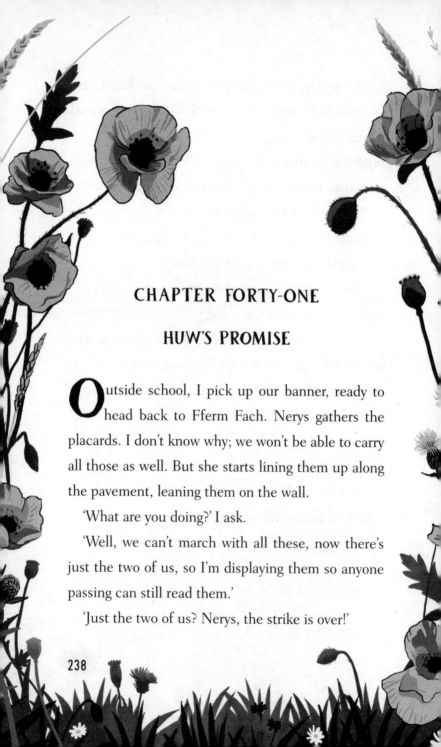

CHAPTER FORTY-ONE

HUW'S PROMISE

Outside school, I pick up our banner, ready to head back to Fferm Fach. Nerys gathers the placards. I don't know why; we won't be able to carry all those as well. But she starts lining them up along the pavement, leaning them on the wall.

'What are you doing?' I ask.

'Well, we can't march with all these, now there's just the two of us, so I'm displaying them so anyone passing can still read them.'

'Just the two of us? Nerys, the strike is over!'

She looks at me like I've lost my mind. 'It's not over! In fact, now Albert and Griff aren't involved, things will go far more smoothly. You watch … the others will come back – and we'll have our demands met in no time.'

'I really don't think it's a good idea.'

'But think about what Charles said – we must never give up.'

I frown. On the field just now with Johnny, we spoke like the clinic in London was the only thing left to try, but it's not – there's still something I can do. Maybe I haven't run out of time after all.

'You're right,' I say.

'Of course I am.' Nerys laughs. 'Now, which placard do you want?'

'No, no, that's not what I meant. Sorry, but I need to go,' I say, backing away. 'Good luck!'

I turn and run as fast as I can up the hill. With each thudding step I feel more and more sure it's the right thing to do. That this is the right time.

I'm going to ask Huw to help Johnny.

*

Huw's standing at the desk, leaning on the back of the chair. He looks up as I burst through the workshop doors. 'That was a very Nerys-style entrance!'

'Sorry,' I pant, trying to get my breath back. 'Can I come in?'

He looks back at the desk. 'Yes, I was just … well … thinking about Rhys.' I walk over. In front of him, next to another letter in the same dainty handwriting, is the wooden pen rest.

Is now the wrong time after all?

But when will there be a right time?

Just do it, Natty.

'Huw?' My heart pounds.

'Yeah?' He wraps the pen rest in its cloth.

'I need your help.'

He glances at me.

'There's another soldier,' I say. Huw stops, his fingers pinching the cloth. 'I met him in the park. He went to war and he's so young. I think he must have lied about his age, like you and Rhys …'

He frowns. 'A lot of us did.'

I scratch at the desktop with my fingernail. 'He can't remember anything.'

'Lucky him.'

'No, you don't understand. He can't remember *anything*. He's got amnesia and doesn't even know who he is. Everyone calls him Johnny but that's not his name.' Huw walks across the workshop and puts the pen rest on the shelf. I follow him. 'But he has a tag … like Rhys's tag … but his is damaged and difficult to read, which is why no one has worked out who he is yet, but I think he might have been in some sort of Guards and, if it was the *Welsh* Guards – Oh, it sounds so stupid now, but – I thought … if you met him … you might know him.'

Huw looks at me like he feels sorry for me. 'Do you know how many boys were in the Welsh Guards?'

My cheeks feel hot. 'I wanted to help him.' I'm shocked at the tears that burst out of me. 'And I thought about you and Rhys and how you said you miss him – and Johnny doesn't even know who's missing him. Or who he should be missing. And we're running out of time.'

Huw leads me back to the chair and sits me down. 'What's all this about?'

'I help him, sometimes.' I sniff. 'He's been remembering little things, and it's because of me.'

Huw smiles. 'That doesn't surprise me.'

'It's just flashes of things, really, but his nurse – she's called Lavinia – she says it's a very good sign. And she says that, because of me, a specialist in London wants to see Johnny, so he's going away.'

Huw twties down in front of me, and squeezes my arm. 'It's good that he's starting to remember, and that you're the one who's helping him, but it sounds like a specialist is exactly what he needs now. There's nothing I can do.'

'I thought it might help you too, to talk to him.'

Huw runs a hand through his hair. 'You can't help everyone. No matter what Aunty Ffion and Nerys might think. Some things can't be mended.'

I nod, taking in big breaths, trying to stop crying. He goes to hand me a cloth to wipe my face but it's covered in paint. Despite everything, we both laugh.

'I'll make you a promise,' Huw says. 'I promise to think about what you've said. Will that do?'

I nod again.

He stands. 'What are you doing home now anyway?'

I huff, my breath coming out strange and wobbly after all the crying. 'Because the strike's off.'

'Oh,' he says. 'I'll put the kettle on. Then you can tell me all about it.'

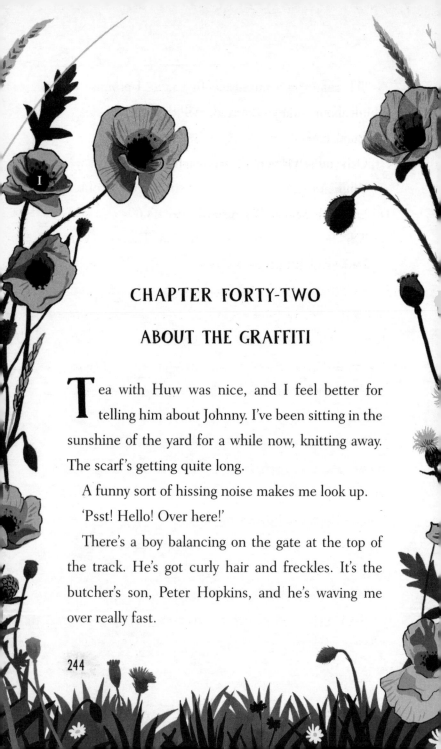

CHAPTER FORTY-TWO

ABOUT THE GRAFFITI

Tea with Huw was nice, and I feel better for telling him about Johnny. I've been sitting in the sunshine of the yard for a while now, knitting away. The scarf's getting quite long.

A funny sort of hissing noise makes me look up.

'Psst! Hello! Over here!'

There's a boy balancing on the gate at the top of the track. He's got curly hair and freckles. It's the butcher's son, Peter Hopkins, and he's waving me over really fast.

'Where's Nerys?' he asks when I reach him.

'Inside, mending our banner. She tried to carry all the signs and—'

'Can you fetch her? Please – and hurry!'

'What? Why?'

'You both need to come with me – it's about the graffiti!'

I'm so shocked, I do as he says.

Soon, we're all off, pelting down the road that runs along the side of the Gweld. Me and Nerys running behind Peter on his delivery bicycle. After a while, the road slopes up and some houses come into view. There are three of them, all big and grand, looking over the valley.

Peter stops with a skid before we reach the first house. We catch up, panting like mad. He leans his bicycle against the garden wall at the side of the house. There are bushes above it.

'Why have you brought us to May Morgan's house?' Nerys asks.

'What?' I say. 'That's May Morgan's house?'

'Sssh!' Peter and Nerys say together.

He leans over, trying to catch his breath. 'I was delivering Councillor Morgan's sausages after school – goes through stacks of them, he does – but when I was getting back on the bicycle, I heard a noise on the path down the side of their house. I pretended I was checking the basket, and saw May, looking around her like she was up to something.'

'She's always up to something,' Nerys says.

'I sneaked round the side and she was putting something in their dustbin, and – well, you'll see.'

'What?' Nerys is almost jumping up and down now. 'What will we see?'

'We just have to wait for – Oh! Here they are.'

Me and Nerys turn to see Owen and Constable Davies coming up the road. It's such a surprise, even Nerys has nothing to say.

'Elias says I ought to look in the Morgans' dustbin, says it's a police matter,' Constable Davies says. 'This had better not be some kind of practical joke.'

'It's not, we promise,' Peter says. He points to his bicycle. 'We'll wait there.'

Constable Davies goes around the front of the big

house and we all duck down by the wall, peering through the bushes. The doorbell chimes, seconds pass, we hear voices.

I catch Owen's eye. He grins. I raise my eyebrows.

Wait and see, he mouths.

Nerys is beside herself.

Then we hear footsteps on the path.

'I honestly have no idea what you could hope to find in our rubbish, Constable, but feel free to investigate our dustbin if you feel you must,' Councillor Morgan says.

'I must,' Davies says.

May appears at the corner of the house just as the policeman lifts the bin lid. 'Daddy! What's he doing? Why's he looking in our dustbin? Tell him to stop!'

But it's too late. Constable Davies is holding up two things. A floppy green hat that looks like a cabbage leaf, and a paintbrush.

Both are covered in white paint.

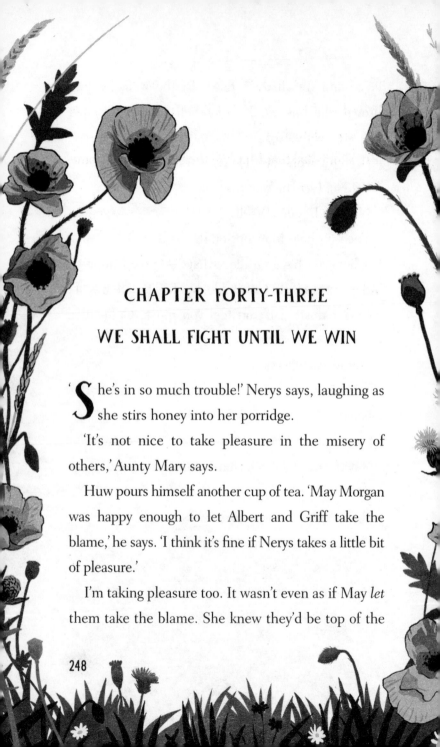

CHAPTER FORTY-THREE

WE SHALL FIGHT UNTIL WE WIN

'She's in so much trouble!' Nerys says, laughing as she stirs honey into her porridge.

'It's not nice to take pleasure in the misery of others,' Aunty Mary says.

Huw pours himself another cup of tea. 'May Morgan was happy enough to let Albert and Griff take the blame,' he says. 'I think it's fine if Nerys takes a little bit of pleasure.'

I'm taking pleasure too. It wasn't even as if May *let* them take the blame. She knew they'd be top of the list of suspects, because of all the things they'd done before. And, because she's a councillor's daughter, no one even thought it might be her. Not even us. I'm just astonished that May had the brains to plan something like this.

'Today's the day then,' Mam says. 'Strike back on.'

'I'll leave you to it.' Huw gets up and goes around the table kissing us all on the top of the head. Nerys giggles. I watch him go out of the door, pleased at this good mood.

'I've fixed your banner,' Uncle Dewi says. 'And I'm proud of you for not giving up.'

'We're not sure anyone else will come though,' I say. 'It might just be me, Nerys and Owen.'

'If you show you have the determination, others will rejoin you, mark my words,' Aunty Mary says. We all look at her. This is the first time she's shown any real support for the strike. 'What?' she says. 'I'm just saying.'

Mam and Nerys smile into their porridge.

Uncle Dewi gets up. 'Right, I'm off to work. Girls, make sure the chickens are happy before you leave. Even revolutionaries have to do their jobs.'

Nerys jumps up. 'Victory to the schoolchildren!'

'After you've collected the eggs.' He kisses Aunty Mary, gives Nerys a big cwtch, then grabs his hat and leaves.

'I'll walk down with you.' Mam looks at me and holds her hands in the air. 'Don't worry, I'm not going to pick up a placard!' She smiles. 'I'm going to see Hannah about something.'

'What thing?' I ask.

'A very good thing,' Mam says. 'Now both of you go and see to the chickens. It'll be quicker with two.'

Owen meets us at the bottom of the track. I'm surprised at how quickly he forgave Nerys for what she said yesterday, but I suppose that's just the way their friendship works. He waves his placard, and reads it out loud. 'WE SHALL FIGHT UNTIL WE WIN. And we will, you know. The likes of the Morgans aren't going to keep thinking they're better than us. Not now.'

'Absolutely,' I say. But as we make our way through the streets of Ynysfach, I start to feel nervous about what might happen today. Mad Dog's going to be madder than ever. May made him look stupid, but

250

he's more likely to take it out on us, even if we aren't actually *in* school.

When we're a few roads away from the high street, the sound of lots of voices reaches us.

'Who's singing at this time of the morning?' Nerys asks

We listen hard as we walk. I don't think it is singing. It sounds more like … We round the corner. The pavement outside school is full of children. And they're chanting.

'What do we want?'

'Free school dinners.'

'When do we want them?'

'NOW!'

And leading the chant is Peter Hopkins. He runs up to us. 'Keep it up!' he shouts over his shoulder to the strikers.

'Peter!' Nerys cries. 'You joined us!'

'I told my father that if vandals and liars are going to school, I'd be in better company out here with you,' he says. 'Then I went and knocked for all these last night –' he waves a hand at the other children – 'and we made new signs in Ivy's shed.'

'They're brilliant,' Owen says, beaming. 'It's all brilliant.'

Everyone has so much energy, the marching is faster, the chanting is louder. Mad Dog rang the bell from the doorway and didn't even look at us. It feels like something's changing. Something we made happen. If this is what it's like to stand up for your rights, then I understand why Mam does it.

At ten o'clock Hannah brings two baskets. There are Welsh cakes, scones, and even a lemon cake. Owen's eyes nearly pop out of his head. He sits with me and Nerys on the pavement, leaning against the school wall.

'I don't know which one to have first,' he says.

The chanting stops and the children crowd round the gate. Something's happening. We get up to see Miss Phillips walking quickly, almost running, across the yard. The little crowd lets us and Peter through to the front.

She opens the gate and looks right at Nerys. 'You can stop now.'

'I'm sorry, miss, but we're not stopping till our

'demands are met,' Nerys says, standing stiff and straight and as tall as she can make herself.

'No, you don't understand.' Miss Phillips puts a hand over her chest, trying to catch her breath. 'You don't have to strike, there's no need—'

'*Miss Phillips*,' Nerys says, like she's the teacher. 'There's every need. Children in this school are hungry. So hungry they can't concentrate on learning. And we're here to change that. Read our banners and placards. We won't give up. Victory to the schoolchildren!' she shouts, and punches the air. Lots of the others copy her.

Miss Phillips holds up her hands and raises her voice. She's smiling. 'Children, children! *Nerys Williams!* This is what I'm trying to tell you. You can stop because you *have* won. The council has agreed to free school dinners.' She looks around at us all. 'You did it, you really did it.'

Nerys turns to me, then Owen. We grab each other and jump up and down. It feels good. Amazing. All around us, the other children cheer and whoop and throw their signs in the air.

'Wait!' Nerys says, pulling away. 'What happened? How did we win?'

'There was a meeting this morning. It seems Councillor Morgan felt he needed to make amends after … erm … the graffiti incident. With his backing – and the backing of Peter's father – your dinners have been won.' She takes a breath, 'Oh, and I'm *so* pleased.'

'My father's the Chair of the Local Chamber of Commerce,' Peter says. 'And no, I don't know what that means either.' He laughs. 'But I made him listen, and *he* made *them* listen.'

'Pack up your signs,' Miss Phillips says. 'It's time to get back to lessons.'

Some of the children groan.

Nerys is first through the gate. 'I hope there's a spelling test.'

'Charles!' I yell, running up the path. 'Charles, you were right!'

An old couple stare at me as I fly past, waving like mad, my satchel banging against my leg. Lavinia,

Johnny and Charles watch me with astonished looks on their faces.

'We did it!' I pant, leaning over the table, rubbing the stitch in my side. 'WE WON THE STRIKE!'

'Bravo!' Charles beams. He claps, and Johnny and Lavinia join in.

I make a low bow, laughing. 'You told us not to give up, Charles, and now we're getting free school dinners!'

'Natty, that's incredible,' Johnny says.

Lavinia looks a bit teary-eyed. 'It really is.'

'See what you can do when you try – you and your cousin and the others?' Charles says, leaning to one side to look past me. 'Where is Nerys, by the way?'

'Stayed behind to do some work for the scholarship exams,' I say. 'She's happy as a sandboy, and I don't even know what a sandboy is but I think I'm as happy as one too!'

Johnny grins. 'Glad to hear it.'

'And you must never give up either,' I say. 'Even when you're in London. *Especially* when you're in London. Promise?'

He nods firmly. 'I promise.'

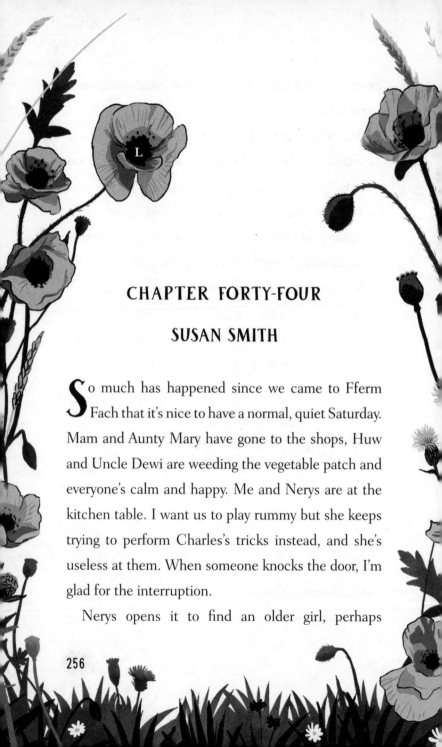

CHAPTER FORTY-FOUR

SUSAN SMITH

So much has happened since we came to Fferm Fach that it's nice to have a normal, quiet Saturday. Mam and Aunty Mary have gone to the shops, Huw and Uncle Dewi are weeding the vegetable patch and everyone's calm and happy. Me and Nerys are at the kitchen table. I want us to play rummy but she keeps trying to perform Charles's tricks instead, and she's useless at them. When someone knocks the door, I'm glad for the interruption.

Nerys opens it to find an older girl, perhaps

eighteen, holding a handbag in front of her, nervously tapping it with her fingers.

She smiles, and that's nervous too.

'Hello,' Nerys says. 'My mam's out, who shall I say called?'

'Hello. Are you Nerys Williams?' the girl asks. 'Have I got the right house?' Her accent is different – might be Carmarthen way.

Nerys shifts about on her feet, nods quickly, and glances back at me.

'My name's Susan Smith,' says the girl.

Where do I know that name from?

Oh!

'Susan Smith? *S. Smith!*' I jump up, banging my legs painfully on the table. 'Like on the envelopes?'

Nerys's face burns red as she stares at the floor. And then I understand why Owen said she was so secretive that day she went to the postbox.

'You wrote to her, didn't you?' I say, rubbing my legs. 'What *the heck* did you do that for?'

Susan looks from Nerys to me.

'Come in,' Nerys says quietly.

We sit at the table, Susan very stiff and straight, her handbag on her lap. She explains that Nerys wrote asking her to visit Huw because of what happened with Sid Davey's gun.

'I didn't know you'd just turn up,' Nerys mumbles.

'I'm sorry,' Susan says. 'Perhaps that wasn't the best idea. But I'm here now.' She looks past me through the living-room door. 'How is Huw?'

'Better,' I say. 'Better than he was.'

Nerys twirls her hair. 'I just thought that, if you're his sweetheart, then you might be the one he needs.'

'Oh! You think I'm *Huw's* ... No, no, no ...' Susan fiddles with the clasp of her handbag. 'I do have a sweetheart, we were to be married straight after the war, but it's not Huw! We just have something in common. Well, some*one*, really. Rhys, my intended.'

Rhys! But Rhys is dead.

'I've never heard of him,' Nerys says, as if she thinks Susan is making it all up.

'No ... well ... that's because they met at Chelsea Barracks and Rhys hasn't ...' She takes a breath. 'Rhys hasn't come home. Yet.'

Nerys frowns. 'What do you mean? Where is he?'

'No one knows.' Susan sits up even straighter, like she's giving a speech she's rehearsed lots of times. 'Before he went missing in action, Rhys wrote to me about his new friend, Huw Williams, so I did some investigating, got some records and found this address. And I wrote to your brother, to see if he knew what happened, and if he could help me find Rhys.'

'And what did he say?' I ask, already knowing the answer.

'Huw thinks he's gone forever, but – if there's no body there's still hope, isn't there?' She leans forward, her eyes flicking between us. Her voice wobbles. '*Missing, presumed dead*, the telegram said. But that's just it, isn't it? It's only *presumed*. It's not a fact.

Missing, presumed dead.

'I didn't know,' I say. 'Huw said Rhys was …'

Nerys turns sharply to face me, and the hurt in her eyes is horrible to see. But she says nothing.

'It's not a fact,' Susan says again.

I think I can feel my heart actually ache, she's so desperate for it to be true. She reaches inside her

259

handbag and takes out an envelope. 'I came to give this to Huw.'

'What's this? Thought my ears were burning.' Huw's in the doorway, taking off his boots. 'Give me what?'

Susan gets to her feet so fast, her handbag drops to the floor. 'Huw.' Her voice is higher than it was before. 'I recognise you from the photograph.'

She steps towards him but he backs away.

'What are you doing here?' he asks.

'So you know me then?'

He nods warily.

Nerys jumps up. 'Huw! We know about Rhys, and Susan's right. You can't give up! Not while there's still a chance he's alive.'

Huw looks at Susan. 'You had no business talking to them. See what you've done?'

'Rhys is my fiancé,' she says, her breathing heavy between words. 'I can talk about him to whoever I like.'

Huw sighs. 'I'm sorry, but you've had a wasted journey. I've already told you. Rhys has gone.'

'And I told you I don't believe it.'

'I wish I could help, I really do. But I've told you everything I know and … if you'd been there, if you'd seen the way it was …' He's looking right at her, but it's as if he's seeing something else. 'Chaos. Boys going over the top like—'

'Huw, please.' She's shaking.

And I think of what he told me about the tapping and the coffins, and I really don't think she would want him to say any more.

He picks his boots back up. 'Look, I know you miss him. I do too.' Huw smiles sadly. 'But he's not coming back.'

He walks off across the yard, boots still in his hand.

Susan picks her handbag off the floor, stares out of the window, and takes a big breath.

'Keep this safe for your brother, eh, Nerys?' She puts the envelope on the table and taps it. 'He'll want to see it.'

'Are you going?' Nerys asks. 'You haven't had a cup of tea.'

'I'll get one at the train station. There's a nice little cafe on the platform.' Susan smiles. 'I think it's best. Today clearly isn't a good day for your brother, but I'll come again. I won't give up.'

We say goodbye.

Nerys flicks the envelope with her finger.

'Don't even think about opening it,' I say.

Her voice is low, full of hurt and hatred, and I know it's because Huw already told me about Rhys. 'Don't you *dare* tell me what to do.' She picks it up. 'I'm going to see my brother.'

'Why don't you leave him alone? You've done enough meddling.'

But she's already gone.

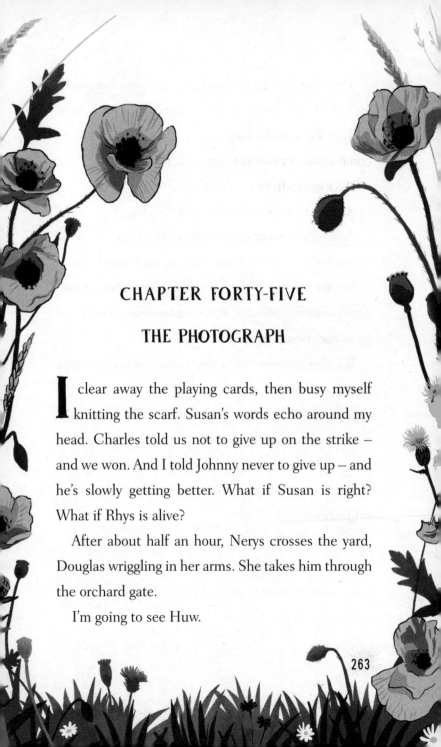

CHAPTER FORTY-FIVE

THE PHOTOGRAPH

I clear away the playing cards, then busy myself knitting the scarf. Susan's words echo around my head. Charles told us not to give up on the strike – and we won. And I told Johnny never to give up – and he's slowly getting better. What if Susan is right? What if Rhys is alive?

After about half an hour, Nerys crosses the yard, Douglas wriggling in her arms. She takes him through the orchard gate.

I'm going to see Huw.

He's standing by the desk, Susan's envelope in his hand.

'Can I come in?' I ask.

He doesn't even look at me, just nods.

I walk over to him. 'What's in it?'

'I don't know.' He holds it out.

A hundred thoughts whirl round my head. What will it be? Will it upset him? Make him happy?

I open the flap and peer inside. 'It's a photograph,' I say quietly, pulling it out. Huw gasps and takes it from me. He stares and stares.

It's of a group of soldiers, about twenty of them. Some standing, some kneeling or sitting on the ground, outside a big stone building. Most of them have caps on, and one holds a rifle, but other than that, it's like a class photograph at school. It might as well be – a lot of the soldiers aren't much older than schoolboys.

'Is that …?' I whisper.

'Me and my mates. Chelsea Barracks.' I glance at him, and am amazed to see he's smiling.

'See if you can find me,' he says.

Even though his face is thinner now, and he looks so much older than the time that's passed, I recognise his dark hair and dark eyes straight away.

'There,' I say, pointing to the one right in the middle.

'That's me,' he says, passing me the photograph. 'And see that fella behind me?'

I look even closer. 'The one with his hand on your shoulder?'

He nods. The soldier's one of the ones without a cap on – his hair's fair and his eyes are pale. And I have to grab the desk to stop myself from falling over. It's Johnny – younger and healthier-looking (just like Huw), but it's Johnny. Huw must know who he is! We can help him! We can …

'Rhys, that is.'

'What?'

'That's Rhys.' He takes the photograph off me, turns it over, points to where the names are written. And the third name in the line marked Row 3 is R.C. Jones. He laughs. 'Just after this photo was taken we all had some whisky that he –' Huw points to a soldier with a neat moustache – 'Fred Matthews, had sneaked in. Thing was, me and Rhys couldn't tell them we'd never had whisky before. We were really sick, threw up everywhere.'

I can't stop staring at Johnny.

'He's gone now, Fred is,' Huw carries on. 'Caught by a shell. That fella there –' he points to the one holding the rifle – 'he was with him, held Fred's hand till he breathed his last. And, do you know what? They never even got on that well.' Huw frowns. 'Doesn't matter in the end though, does it?' He looks at me. 'Out of all of us, only six came back.'

I can't take all this in – the young soldiers, the deaths they faced, the fact that Huw's wrong. It's not six, it's seven.

And it's like the workshop is a ship, and it's rolling and rocking on the waves, making my head whoosh. Because now I get it. Now I know.

Rhys is Johnny.

Johnny is Rhys.

I watch Huw, my heart pounding out of my chest.

His eyes narrow. 'You all right, there? You look like you've seen a ghost.'

I have to tell him. I can't tell him. But how can I not?

'That's Johnny, the soldier I told you about – the one in the park.'

'What? Where?'

I point at Rhys.

'Don't be daft, mun. I just told you that's Rhys.'

'Yes,' I say slowly. 'And Rhys is Johnny.'

Huw stares at me forever, like he's trying to see right into me, his dark eyes confused. He pulls out the chair and sits, elbows on the desk, his hands in his hair.

What have I done? What if I've made him ill again?

When Huw looks up, his eyes are wet. His voice is a whisper. 'You could be mistaken.'

I twty down next to him and put a hand on his arm. Just like he did with me when I was upset. Just like Johnny did. With the other, I pick up the photograph and look again at Johnny, my friend from the park. 'I'm not.'

267

'You still could be.' He makes fists, and his hair sticks up through his fingers in little tufts.

'Where was Rhys from?' I ask.

'Carmarthen.'

'Johnny's got a Carmarthen accent.'

'So have lots of people.'

'Huw, it's him. It's really him.'

He looks right at me. 'Get my dad.'

Uncle Dewi's in the scullery. He glances at me, then turns back to the shelves. 'Your sister never puts things back in their proper place,' he says.

'My sister?'

'Oh, hark at me!' He laughs. 'We're so used to you now, Natty.' He drops a scrubbing brush into a metal bucket. 'Did you want me for something?'

'Not me – Huw.'

He frowns. 'Everything all right?'

'I don't know.'

Uncle Dewi runs out of the kitchen and across the yard.

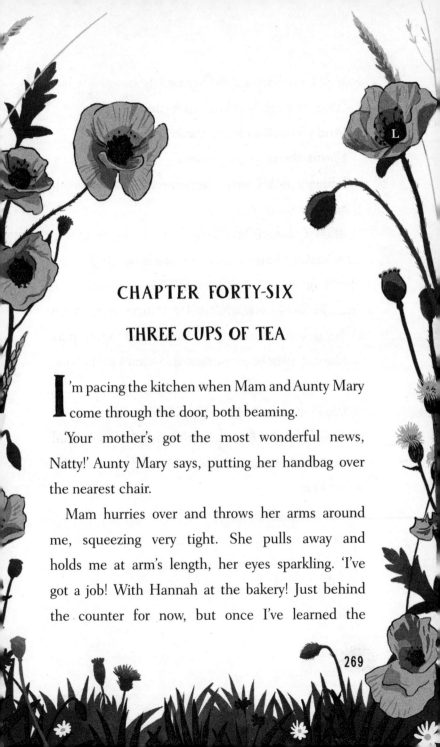

CHAPTER FORTY-SIX

THREE CUPS OF TEA

I'm pacing the kitchen when Mam and Aunty Mary come through the door, both beaming.

'Your mother's got the most wonderful news, Natty!' Aunty Mary says, putting her handbag over the nearest chair.

Mam hurries over and throws her arms around me, squeezing very tight. She pulls away and holds me at arm's length, her eyes sparkling. 'I've got a job! With Hannah at the bakery! Just behind the counter for now, but once I've learned the ropes I can help with the baking.'

'That's good news,' I say, trying to look happy.

'And you haven't heard the best part yet.'

She waits, obviously wanting me to ask, but my mind is too full of Huw and Johnny – who isn't really Johnny at all.

She lets me go. 'Well, you could show a little more enthusiasm, Natty. I thought you'd be landed. You like Hannah, and it seemed like you were starting to enjoy living in Ynysfach.'

'It's not that, Mam.'

She tilts her head on one side, and speaks more gently. 'What is it then? What's the matter?'

I look at Aunty Mary. 'Uncle Dewi's in the work-shop with Huw. He's all right!' I say quickly. 'I mean, it's not shell shock again but … well … you need to go to them.'

She throws her shopping bag on the table and rushes off.

Mam runs the back of her hand lightly over my cheek. 'I'll put the kettle on,' she says.

We sit holding hands across the table. Mam listens

without saying a word. Sometimes she nods or squeezes my hand as I tell her about Huw and Rhys and the soldiers in the park. When I get to the part where Susan visited, she puts her other hand over her heart and I know she's thinking about Dad. It takes three cups of tea each to say it all.

Then we just sit, sometimes looking out across the yard to the workshop.

'Well done on getting the job, Mam,' I say.

She smiles. 'Thanks, love.'

'You can tell me the best part now.'

Mam leans closer. 'We've got somewhere to live too. Hannah says we can have the flat over the shop. I've seen it, and it's lovely. There's a bedroom each and Hannah's going to spruce it up just for us! Isn't that kind?'

'That's brilliant!' I say. 'Hannah's always kind.'

I picture Mam in the bakery, serving bread and cakes and chatting to customers. She'll be good at that.

'You've done so much since we came here,' she says suddenly. 'Helping Johnny, helping Huw, the strike. All those years I tried to get you to be like me … I thought it would bring us close again – like when you were a little girl – because, well, I missed that. But now I can see I should have just let you find your own way.'

I shrug. 'Perhaps I'm a bit more like you than I thought.'

Mam scrunches up her face. 'And is that so bad?'

'I'll let you know when I've got used to the idea.'

She laughs, and pulls me to her for a big cwtch.

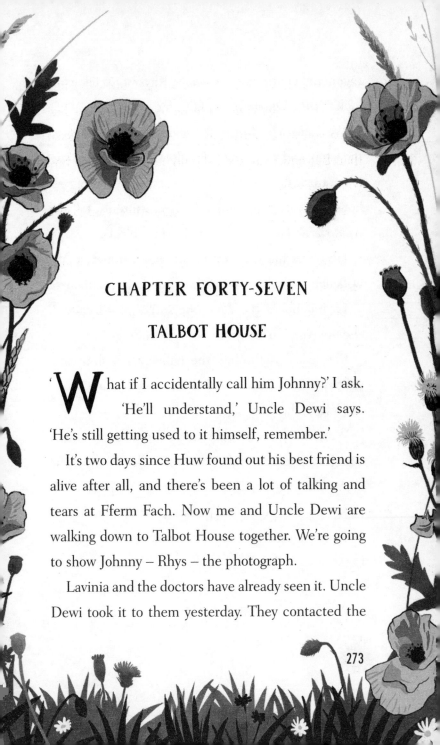

CHAPTER FORTY-SEVEN

TALBOT HOUSE

'What if I accidentally call him Johnny?' I ask.

'He'll understand,' Uncle Dewi says. 'He's still getting used to it himself, remember.'

It's two days since Huw found out his best friend is alive after all, and there's been a lot of talking and tears at Fferm Fach. Now me and Uncle Dewi are walking down to Talbot House together. We're going to show Johnny – Rhys – the photograph.

Lavinia and the doctors have already seen it. Uncle Dewi took it to them yesterday. They contacted the

273

regiment, confirmed it's really Rhys. But he won't look at the photograph without me.

We stand in front of the big gates. Uncle Dewi opens the latch, and we go through. I look up at the building. It's not exactly a mansion, but it must be the biggest house for miles. It's grand, with white walls, tall bay windows and a porch held up by thick pillars.

He offers me his arm. I link mine through it. We walk across the gravel forecourt and he rings the bell.

Lavinia opens the door. She smiles, but I can tell she's nervous. 'Thank you both for coming.'

She leads us through the hallway. It's shiny and echoey, with a huge wooden staircase leading up on our left, and closed doors on both sides.

We go along a corridor. A nurse comes out of another door further down, and as we pass, I glance inside the room. There are beds, and men in stripy pyjamas. It looks odd with all the old paintings on the walls.

'There aren't as many patients as there were,' Lavinia says. 'Thankfully most have been able to go home. Some have to go to other institutions, as we can't stay open indefinitely.'

274

She stops us before we go through an open archway. 'There are a couple of things I need you to know. Rhys's parents have been informed, and will be here later today. We all think it's best if that happens before he's told about Susan. She's agreed to wait. So please don't mention her.'

'Is he still going to London?' I ask.

'It's postponed for now. We'll see how it goes once Rhys has met his family.'

Postponed. So it's still possible.

We go through into a long room, which must run all along the back of the house. Sunshine pours in through huge, arched windows. There are men in the same Hospital Blues that Johnny and Charles wear, sitting in big leather chairs or around tables playing chess. Some, like Charles, look wounded. They have missing limbs or scars. For others it's only the uniform which shows they're unwell. And there, sitting near a window, looking out over the garden, is Johnny.

Rhys.

He turns, sees us and jumps up quickly. He's

shaking worse than ever, and I want to run over and cwtch him like Nerys does with Huw. But I don't.

Lavinia introduces Uncle Dewi, and we all sit in those big leather chairs around a low table laid with a jug of cordial and a plate of garibaldi biscuits. I sit back in my chair and feel tiny.

The silence is awful.

So I break it.

'Do you want to see the photograph?'

Lavinia looks startled. 'Natty, perhaps we should have some refreshments and then—'

'No,' Rhys says. 'Let's not.' He holds out a shaking hand.

Uncle Dewi reaches into his pocket for the envelope. 'Here you go, boy.'

We all watch as Rhys takes out the photograph of the group of soldiers at Chelsea Barracks. He stares and stares, and it feels like forever.

'Can you remember it being taken?' Lavinia asks quietly.

Rhys shakes his head.

'Can you remember being at the barracks?'

Rhys shakes his head again.

'What about the other soldiers? Can you remember any of them?'

He still doesn't take his eyes from the photograph. 'I've got my hand on this one's shoulder. Who's he?'

I lean forward. 'That's Huw!'

Next to me, Uncle Dewi breathes in sharply.

Rhys looks up. 'And we were best mates?'

'Yes,' I say. 'Do you remember?'

'No.' He puts the photograph back in the envelope and rubs his eyes. 'But he's got a kind face.'

The words burst out of me. 'Will you come and see Huw? Come to Fferm Fach?'

'Natty,' Lavinia says with a briskness in her voice. 'I know you mean well, but we really must stick to procedure—'

'I'll come,' Rhys says firmly.

Lavinia's lips go tight. She looks from Rhys to me. 'I'll speak to the doctors. Will that do?'

We both nod.

'Now,' she says in her strictest nurse voice. 'This is clearly too much for one visit. Rest for you, young man.'

Lavinia walks me and Uncle Dewi out of the sunny room, but at the archway, I stop.

'Oh! I almost forgot!'

I run back to Rhys and reach into my bulging pocket.

'I made you this.' I hold out the woolly red scarf. 'I know the weather's getting warmer, but it's all I can make, and I thought perhaps you could save it for winter. It's nice and cwtchy and soft and, if you wrap it a certain way, the holes don't show.'

I stop, slightly breathless. I must sound like Nerys, going on and on.

Rhys takes the scarf and squeezes it. 'Nice and cwtchy and soft,' he says quietly. 'Thank you, Natty.'

And I give him that cwtch – the one like a sister gives a brother.

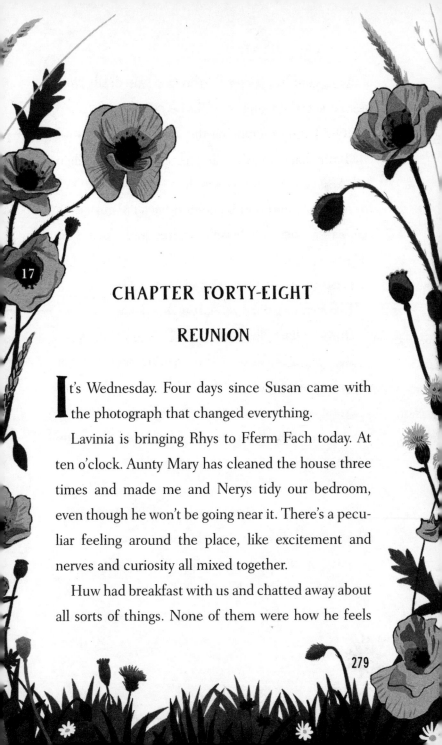

CHAPTER FORTY-EIGHT

REUNION

It's Wednesday. Four days since Susan came with the photograph that changed everything.

Lavinia is bringing Rhys to Fferm Fach today. At ten o'clock. Aunty Mary has cleaned the house three times and made me and Nerys tidy our bedroom, even though he won't be going near it. There's a peculiar feeling around the place, like excitement and nerves and curiosity all mixed together.

Huw had breakfast with us and chatted away about all sorts of things. None of them were how he feels about seeing the friend he thought was dead. Now he's pacing the living room in his Sunday best, and Aunty Mary is rearranging the scullery shelves with Mam.

Uncle Dewi's doing jobs in the yard. Nerys watches from the kitchen window, holding back the curtain to see better. The sunlight reflects deep pink flowers on to her face.

'What time is it?' she asks, not looking round.

'Two minutes since you last asked,' I say.

'Don't be horrible, Natty.'

She's right. Now's not the time to be sarcastic. 'I'm sorry. It's five to ten.'

'Not long now,' she whispers. 'I hope they're on time. I hope Rhys hasn't changed his mind.' She turns to me, wide-eyed, and the curtain drops back into place. 'You don't think he will, do you?'

'Nerys, be quiet.' Aunty Mary is in the doorway to the scullery. 'This *will not* help your brother.'

'Sorry, Mam,' she says, then turns back to the window. She gasps. 'They're here!'

Aunty Mary blinks, then takes a very big breath.

She lets it out slowly. 'You girls go out, so Rhys sees friendly and familiar faces, like Lavinia said, and I'll wait with Huw.'

Me and Nerys hold hands and leave the kitchen. Uncle Dewi's letting them through the gate.

Rhys sees us and waves. He's smiling, it's only tiny, but it's still a smile. That has to be a good sign. We walk across the yard to meet them. Nerys keeps doing little skips, and I can tell she just wants to run.

'You live in a very nice place,' Rhys says, looking around the smallholding and up at the Gweld. The sun's on his face and his lashes are almost invisible.

'We can show you the pigs after,' Nerys says. 'And Ginty – she's our goat – and we have lots of chickens. And an orchard.'

Uncle Dewi puts an arm around her. 'Maybe another day, eh, love?'

'Where's Huw?' Rhys asks, and it seems so sudden, even though that's why he's here, that my stomach squeezes up tight.

Uncle Dewi smiles in that nice, kind way he does. 'I'll go and fetch him now, boy.' He looks into Rhys's face, and his eyebrows scrunch down. 'If you're ready?'

But Huw's already at the back door. The two boys walk towards each other until they meet in the middle of the yard. We follow so far, and then stop. Aunty Mary and Mam watch from the doorway. I don't think any of us knows what else to do.

Huw holds out a hand. Rhys takes it, then Huw puts his other hand on Rhys's shoulder and they look at each other.

'It's really you,' Huw says, his voice just a scratchy whisper.

'Is it?' Rhys asks.

'Yes.'

Rhys looks around. 'Your sister says you've got pigs.'

Huw nods.

'Can I see them?'

They walk towards the sty. Aunty Mary rushes over to us. 'Will they be all right on their own?'

'I'll give them some time, then check on them,' Lavinia says. 'Don't worry, Mrs Williams, it'll be fine.'

Aunty Mary nods, not taking her eyes off the boys.

'Tell you what,' Lavinia says gently. 'Let's get Nerys and Natty to make a pot of tea, and we'll sit out here and drink it, shall we? Nice and close.'

'There's cake too,' Aunty Mary says, talking like she's in a dream, still watching Huw and Rhys. 'I made bara brith.'

CHAPTER FORTY-NINE

TOGETHER AGAIN

'They're leaning on the fence,' Nerys says from the kitchen window. 'They're talking – well, Huw's talking – and … Oh! I think he's showing Rhys how to scratch the pigs on the head, the way they like it. Rhys is smiling, Natty! I can see from here.'

I put down the sugar bowl and go to stand with her.

She grins. 'This is the best day since we won the strike.'

'It is.' No matter what happens next, Huw and Rhys are together again.

Mam appears in the doorway. 'Need a hand?'

The three of us take out the tea and bara brith, and set it all on the little table. We sit, pretending not to watch Huw and Rhys, but not being able to help it.

Aunty Mary's jittery. She keeps lifting her cup, saying the tea's too hot to drink, and that she's a silly thing, and putting it back down again. Nerys pulls her chair right next to her and they cwtch up. Uncle Dewi eats three slices of cake.

Huw and Rhys walk away from the sty and over to the workshop.

Lavinia turns to Aunty Mary, who looks like she's about to throw Nerys off and run after them. 'Best to leave them be.' Lavinia sips her tea. 'Now, girls, tell me all about this strike.'

It's the perfect distraction for Nerys. She especially likes talking about how May Morgan was caught. She's just at the part where we saw Peter and the others with their placards when Huw calls down the yard.

'Did you say there was bara brith?'

Nerys leaps up. 'We'll bring it!'

Aunty Mary gets up too. 'I really think me and your father ought to go,' she says.

'No, Mam, let Nerys and Natty,' Huw says. 'We want to show them something.'

Uncle Dewi puts a hand on Aunty Mary's arm. 'I'll freshen the pot, take it up in a few minutes.'

Nerys piles about half the cake on to a plate. 'I wonder what they want to show us,' she says.

At the workshop door, Huw rushes over and pulls us across to where Rhys is sitting at the desk, bent over something. 'I showed him. He doesn't remember it, but look – look what's he's doing!'

Rhys is holding a smooth block of wood with grooves in the top. The pen rest. He pushes a chisel into its surface.

'He remembers how to carve!' Huw says.

'I remember the pattern too,' Rhys says quietly, not looking up. 'These flowers … and the stems … the way they swirl.'

'Isn't it amazing?' Huw breathes.

I nod because I can't speak.

'That's beautiful,' Nerys says. 'It looks like a pen

rest – is it a pen rest? Miss Phillips has got one on her desk. It's not as lovely as this though.'

Huw puts an arm around her. 'I'm glad you like it, because it's for you. It was meant to be a surprise, but that doesn't seem to matter now.'

'Really? Oh, thank you!' She cuddles him tight. 'But I don't understand. How does Rhys know how to make the pattern?'

'Because he designed it,' Huw says.

She stares at her brother.

'The pen rest was Rhys's idea. We started it in the trenches in Belgium.'

Nerys looks back at Rhys. 'Oh.'

He holds up the block. 'And, here, in the middle, this is where your initials will go, Nerys. See?'

Huw makes a funny sort of gasp and turns away, his hand over his face. When he turns back, he's wiping tears from his cheeks. 'You remembered! But how?'

'I don't know,' Rhys says, a smile on his face like I've never seen. 'I don't know *how* I know. I just do.'

'I love it,' Nerys says. 'And I'll use it every day when I'm at the Brecon County School.'

'You have to get your scholarship first,' I tease.

She pulls a face as if to say *Why wouldn't I?* and me and Huw laugh.

'Well, this is a lovely sound,' Uncle Dewi says from the doorway. 'All the young ones having fun.' He holds up a tray. 'Your mam seems to think you'll die of thirst unless you have this.'

'Bring it in,' Huw says. 'We'll have it now in a minute. Come and see this, Dad.'

Uncle Dewi does as he's asked, and watches in wonder as Rhys carves a long, curling stem.

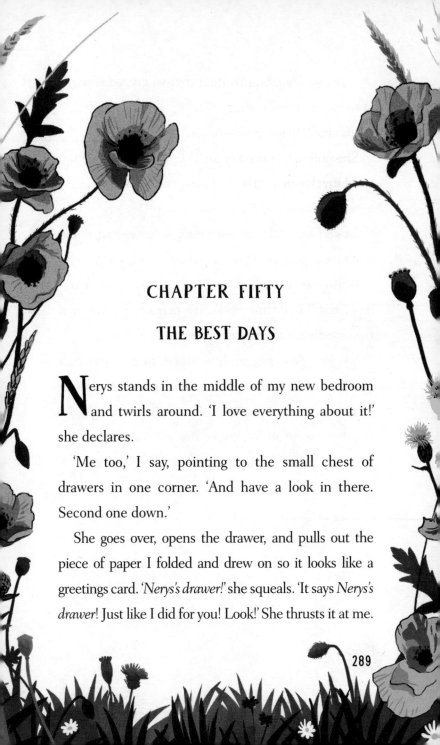

CHAPTER FIFTY

THE BEST DAYS

Nerys stands in the middle of my new bedroom and twirls around. 'I love everything about it!' she declares.

'Me too,' I say, pointing to the small chest of drawers in one corner. 'And have a look in there. Second one down.'

She goes over, opens the drawer, and pulls out the piece of paper I folded and drew on so it looks like a greetings card. '*Nerys's drawer!*' she squeals. 'It says *Nerys's drawer*! Just like I did for you! Look!' She thrusts it at me.

'I know.' I laugh. 'I wrote it! For when you come to stay.'

'Really?'

'Yes.'

'Even though it's the first time you've had a room of your very own?'

'Yes! It's half the drawer, really, but we can share, can't we?'

She flings herself at me and squeezes very tight. 'It's going to be wonderful! We can stay up late and have midnight feasts and pillow fights and—'

'We never did any of those things in your house!'

She steps away, looking suddenly serious. 'That's because it's not the same. This will be like I'm on holiday, except in Ynysfach. But anyway, it won't be *quite* so lonely without you because Douglas is coming to live with us.'

'Douglas?'

'Yes. Sid Davey said he's always escaping to Fferm Fach so he may as well be our dog, and Mam said no, but I went to Dad and told him how sad I'll be on my own again, and he convinced her, so – Douglas is going to be mine! He'll take your place in the bed.'

I think Aunty Mary might have something to say about that, but I let Nerys have her daydream.

We sit on the bed and talk and talk. Sometimes I even get a word in. Uncle Dewi took Huw to Talbot House to meet Rhys's mam and dad. Rhys doesn't remember them. He doesn't remember anyone yet, but the doctors are hopeful. Susan came yesterday. Even though Rhys doesn't know her as his sweetheart, she made a joke and he laughed and no one else understood it, only them.

'I think he knows he loves her,' Nerys says.

Mam pops her head around the door. 'Tea's ready.' We sit at the table in our new living room, with daffs in a vase in the middle. Aunty Mary pours, and we have a tin of Huntley and Palmers assorted cream biscuits, because it's an extra-special day.

From my bedroom window, I look down at the pavement where we marched and chanted and argued and ate and laughed and won.

In the distance, I can just make out the roof of the

bowling pavilion. Johnny knows he's Rhys now, even if he doesn't remember yet. Tomorrow, I'll go and see Charles and Lavinia.

'Here you are, love,' Mam calls. I go into the passage, where she's waiting for me, holding out some money. 'I'll butter the bread.'

I take the coins, and grin at her. 'This feels different, doesn't it, Mam? It feels like it's going to last.'

She nods and smiles. 'It really does.'

I go out of our front door and down the stairs. On the street, I turn left and head up the hill.

Towards the chippy.

THERE'S ONE MORE MYSTERY TO UNRAVEL ...

Have you ever heard of an anagram? It's when a word, phrase or name can be made by rearranging the letters of another one. For example, SCHOOLMASTER is an anagram of THE CLASSROOM, but let's not think about Mad Dog Manford right now! Maybe you like unscrambling anagrams or even inventing them ... Well, there's one hidden in the pages of this story, just for you!

It's one that Natty would have liked to solve – to help Johnny. And if you want to have a go at working it out, *I* can help *you* ...

Take a close look at the poppies at the beginning of each chapter and you'll find some hidden letters and numbers. When you put them all together in the order they appear throughout the book, they make a sentence. But this sentence is an anagram, so you need to unscramble it to work out what it *really* means.

I'll give you a clue. Flick back to the picture on page 57 and think about what's missing. Could you be the one to solve this mystery? I hope so!

Good luck!

lesley

ACKNOWLEDGEMENTS

I'd like to send my huge thanks to:

My fantastic editor Zöe Griffiths and all at Bloomsbury Children's, especially Beatrice Cross, Jade Westwood and Fliss Stevens – I'm so proud to be part of this team.

Amber Caravéo, my marvellous agent.

Illustrator David Dean and designer Jet Purdie for another gorgeous cover.

All the booksellers, bloggers, reviewers, librarians, teachers and TAs who have supported me and my books.

Leigh Barnard and Andy Duckhouse for your generosity and openness in helping me research PTSD and amnesia, respectively.

All the friends who have cheered me on, lifted me up and made me feel like a second book was actually possible.

Deborah, for being the best of the best.

Jon ... for endless and unwavering support.

And last, but never least, my readers.

HAVE YOU READ

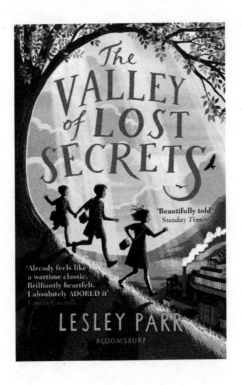

A timeless historical mystery about

brotherhood and bravery

AVAILABLE NOW

Turn the page for a sneak peek …

CHAPTER ONE

A DIFFERENT TYPE OF COUNTRYSIDE

There isn't as much sky as I thought there'd be. And what I can see is clear and blue, not the never-ending rain clouds we were told we'd get in Wales.

The guard blows his whistle and the train hoots back. I watch it pull away and my heart squeezes a bit. I want to get back on. I don't know why; it's not as if it's going back to London.

We've been through three stations today – from Paddington to Cardiff Central to here. This one's tiny, with only one platform. It's like our lives are shrinking. I straighten Ronnie's tag and we join the back of the line.

Dad said we'd be able to see for miles and miles in the countryside. He got us some library books with pictures of fields and hedgerows with little houses dotted around. But this isn't like that.

Massive, looming bulges of land – mountains, I suppose – have stolen most of the sky. I turn on the spot. They're all around, as though the village was dropped into the middle of a big fat cushion. Before now, the closest thing to a mountain I'd ever seen was a sand dune on Camber Sands. And it wasn't green. And it didn't have houses stuck on the side of it.

There's a tug at my sleeve. Ronnie's looking at me, eyes wide and teary. I lean down so he can whisper in my ear.

'This isn't like the pictures,' he says, sniffing.

'I know.'

'But Dad said—'

'He didn't know, did he? He didn't know we were coming here. He just knew it wasn't a city.' I look around again. 'There must be different types of countryside.'

'Well, this is the wrong type.' Ronnie sticks out his bottom lip.

This is all I need – a sulky little brother. No one will pick us if he looks a proper misery guts.

'Be quiet and try to look like a nice boy,' I say, making sure the string of his gas mask box sits properly on his shoulder. 'Nice and smart.'

I look over his head to the far end of the platform. The smoke's thinning, but it still stings my eyes and catches in my throat. I can see the face of the station clock now; it's almost teatime. The sign is clear too:

LLANBRYN

Funny word. Too many Ls.

Here we are, a wriggling, squiggling line of school-children. Duff's at the front with his little sister. She's even younger than Ronnie; too young to understand any of this. I can't see many faces; most are looking at our teacher, Miss Goodhew. Some of us seem excited,

3

some curious, but I bet everyone's nervous. Even the ones pretending not to be. Maybe even Duff.

Ronnie's crying again. It's OK for little brothers to cry but big brothers have to be the brave ones. Not that I would cry, anyway. I'm twelve. He watches sadly as a guard puts our suitcases in a pile near the gate at the end of the platform.

'I want my Dinky van,' he splutters.

'You can't have it. It's packed. You know what Nan said.'

'But—'

'Ronnie, it's safe,' I say. 'Remember how well you wrapped it in your pyjamas? You did a really good job there.'

He nods and blinks back more tears. I know he's trying to be brave too.

Next to the guard, Miss Goodhew is talking to a man and a woman. The man is tall and has a thick overcoat buttoned over his large stomach, and he's got the biggest moustache I've ever seen. The woman's all done up like she's in her Sunday best. She's walking down the line now, giving out custard creams as she

4

counts us. When she gives one to Lillian Baker, Lillian thanks her for having us in their village. Duff's close enough to pull her plaits but he doesn't. He's not usually worried about getting into trouble; perhaps he *is* nervous. I bet Lillian Baker will get picked first. She's got long dark hair and her socks never fall down and all the grown-ups say she's pretty.

When the woman hands a biscuit to Ronnie, she stops and wipes away his tears with her hanky. She's got a metal badge pinned to her coat that says *WVS Housewives Service Identification*.

'What's your name?' she asks. Ronnie gulps and says nothing.

Now that she's close, I can smell lavender and peppermints. She lifts Ronnie's tag and says, 'Ronald, now that's one of my favourite names, that is.'

'We call him Ronnie,' I say, a bit harder than I mean to.

But she keeps on smiling, eyeing my tag. 'And you're a Travers too. Ronnie's brother, is it? So are you a James or a Jimmy?'

'Jimmy.'

'All right then,' she says. She gives me a custard cream and moves back up the line.

'She smells like Nan,' Ronnie whispers. His lip's wobbling again, so I take his hand and give it a squeeze, just like Dad would do.

'Eat your biscuit,' I say.

Miss Goodhew claps her hands and calls out to us. We all go quiet.

'These nice people are Mr and Mrs Bevan,' she shouts down the platform, using her fake-posh voice. 'They are here to take us up to the institute.'

I wonder what an institute is. It sounds grim.

'Welcome to Llanbryn!' Mr Bevan booms. I'm not surprised he booms. He looks like a boomer.

I glance at the sign again. It doesn't look like it says what *he* just said. Ronnie's copying him, screwing up his face, trying to make his mouth fit around the letters.

'Lll … clll … cllaaa …'

'Stop it,' I whisper. 'No one will pick us if they think you're simple.'

'Don't worry about your cases,' Mr Bevan says. 'We've got men taking them up for you.'

Ronnie tightens his grip on my hand and I know he's thinking about his Dinky van again. Those men – whoever they are – had better be careful with his case. If he loses that van, he won't stop crying till the end of the war.

We set off, our gas mask boxes bumping against us. Mrs Bevan and Miss Goodhew chat at the head of the line. Mr Bevan waits as we cross the road outside the station, then joins Ronnie and me at the back.

'Are you ready for your adventure, boys?' he asks, grinning.

What's he talking about? Adventures happen in jungles or on raging rivers or in the Wild West. Not here. Not in Wales with a whimpering little brother and a custard cream.

Ronnie's stopped crying, so that's something. He's twisted the top off his biscuit and is licking the creamy bit.

'Are we going up there?' he asks, his eyes darting nervously from Mr Bevan to the mountainside houses.

Mr Bevan nods. 'We are.'

'It's a long way up,' Ronnie says.

Mr Bevan turns to the houses and tilts his head from side to side. A big grin breaks out on his face, stretching his moustache and making him look like a happy walrus.

'Not for a big strong boy like you!'

Ronnie beams.

'Come on then!' Mr Bevan ruffles Ronnie's hair. I smooth it down again. No one will pick us if he looks a proper mess. I might not want to be here, but I don't fancy us being the last ones chosen, either – the dregs in the bottom of a bottle.

We start to climb a wide track. Bushes and trees grow on either side. Ronnie asks if it's a forest. I catch Mr Bevan's eye and see his moustache twitch over his smile.

'Stop asking stupid questions,' I hiss in Ronnie's ear.

Then, up ahead, Duff's little sister drops her custard cream. She stops dead and just stays there until her face turns a greyish shade of blue. I've seen her do this lots of times before, when we've been out playing, but Mr Bevan looks horrified.

'What's she doing?' he asks.

'Holding her breath,' I answer. 'She can only do it for so long, then she really starts.'

'Starts what?'

'Wait for it.'

I don't know if it's got anything to do with the mountains curving all round us, but her wails are even louder here, not far off an air-raid siren. The two women rush over to her and Mrs Bevan opens her handbag. She feels around inside, pulls out a chocolate bar and snaps off a piece.

'Dairy Milk,' Ronnie groans. 'I should've dropped *my* biscuit.'

As we move off, Florence Campbell picks up the custard cream and stuffs it in her pocket. I pretend not to see. I don't think Florence can believe her luck – two biscuits in one day. I bet she's never had two biscuits in her whole life.

We keep climbing until we reach another road. We follow it round the corner until an enormous brown-brick building comes into view. It's three storeys high, bulky and strong-looking.

9

'I'll just catch up with Miss Goodhew and my wife at the front,' Mr Bevan says. 'You two wait by here.'

'Jimmy calls her Miss Badhew,' Ronnie says, 'because she isn't nice, so she can't be a *good* hew, can she?'

'Ronnie!' I mutter.

But Mr Bevan is laughing. 'Don't worry, Jimmy. We had nicknames for teachers when I was a boy too.'

He walks away and I can't believe I haven't been told off.

'Here we are,' he says, standing in the arched doorway. He looks really proud, like he's showing us Buckingham Palace. 'The Llanbryn Miners Institute.'

I look from Mr Bevan to the institute. They match, the way some people do with their dogs. There's something about him that says he belongs here, like he's a part of this place. But that just makes me feel even more like an outsider.

'Everyone's in the main hall. They can't wait to see you.'

The room is massive, much bigger than our school hall. It's all dark timber, polished up till it shines.

There are steps and a raised platform at the far end, a bit like a stage. The room's bursting with people all staring and muttering; surely they can't all want an evacuee? Some must be here to gawp. They sit in rows in front of the platform and, as we walk past them to the raised bit, I can feel the place swallowing us up – my little brother, all the others and me.

ABOUT THE AUTHOR

Lesley grew up in South Wales and now lives in England with her husband and their rescue cat, Angharad. She shares her time between writing stories, teaching at a primary school and tutoring adults. Apart from books, rugby union is her favourite thing in the world, especially if Wales is winning. Lesley graduated with distinction from Bath Spa University's MA in Writing for Young People. *When the War Came Home* is her second novel.

@WelshDragonParr